BEST FRIENDS

Also by Andrew Meehan

One Star Awake
The Mystery of Love
Instant Fires

BEST FRIENDS

Andrew Meehan

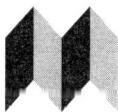

MUSWELL
PRESS

First published by Muswell Press in 2025
Copyright © Andrew Meehan 2025

Typeset in Bembo by M Rules
Printed by CPI Group (UK) Ltd, Croydon CR0 4YY

A CIP record for this book is available from the British Library

ISBN: 9781068684432
eISBN: 9781068684449

Muswell Press, London N6 5HQ
www.muswell-press.co.uk

Our authorised representative in the EU for product safety is
Easy Access System Europe, Mustamäe tee 50, 10621 Tallinn, Estonia
gpsr.requests@easproject.com

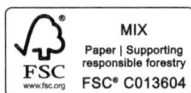

For Áine Prendergast.

Come then, your ways and airs and
looks, locks, maiden gear, gallantry and
gaiety and grace,
    Winning ways, airs innocent,
maiden manners, sweet looks, loose
locks, long locks, lovelocks, gaygear,
going gallant, girlgrace—
    Resign them, sign them, seal them,
send them, motion them with breath,
    And with sighs soaring, soaring síghs
deliver
    Them; beauty-in-the-ghost, deliver
it, early now, long before death
    Give beauty back, beauty, beauty,
beauty, back to God, beauty's self and
beauty's giver.

from 'The Leaden Echo and the Golden
Echo' by Gerard Manley Hopkins

1

Jars

June goes to bed early.

The machinery you hear in the night, all the little rumbles that reach the heart, at her age everything ends up there. When it gets too much all you can do is get up again.

She has made a little pact with herself.

If it's a nice day, get out in it.

But every week that passes, this village becomes far too five-star in itself. Some of the houses on the seafront are so smartened up that they look refrigerated, they've gotten rid of all the seaweed smells and the sewage smells, anything that sends out the wrong information. June is the wrong information.

She makes her way up the most immaculate driveway—the gravel is like something you'd put on ice-cream, the windows have a Dracula sheen to them—and she wants to know what it is like for rich people to be the way they are, which is what? Strange. But nothing in life is as straight-forward as it should be.

June Wylie's seventy-four years old and going door to door looking for jam jars for her honey.

June can be a funny one, with all its scattered light and the stretching of the days. And this has been a very funny June, not even midsummer and the daisies are flopping, it's criminal how even the roses are too tired to open up. Too much effort required.

The bay first thing this morning was looking divine, and June would really like this June to be a bit less divine. A bit less deluxe. She'd like everything to be a bit more low-key.

June needs June to be little less and little more.

She'd like not to be in these socks, woollen and speaking of winter, she'd like to have her legs out, as if it's 1956 and she's been climbing down from the most ancient oak tree in Helen's Bay, and as if it's 1977 and she's been drinking bottles of export Guinness on the Regent's canal, and as if it's 2002 and she can't get out of bed (the bad memories you can't remember any more, they're the worst), none of which has much bearing on the way things have been lately, which is not very bare legs-like at all.

Young is anyone under the age of June's age, and the young woman who answers the door is as refrigerated as her house.

—Just wondering if you have any empty jars? June says.

—Why would I have jars? the young woman says.

—Jam jars.

—Why would I have jam?

The woman is affronted at the very mention of anything containing sugar. And why would she have jam, indeed?

For all June knows, this woman might have strong feelings on the subject.

For all June knows, this might be a bad time, jam-wise, life-wise. For all June knows this woman has three ex-husbands, too.

The woman starts padding around the place like she's Princess Caroline of Monaco. It's an open-plan semi, June's cleaned plenty of those, and she is, of course, thinking of the price of everything—five grand couches, cutlery to put yours to shame—and the fact that cleaning such nice houses reminds you of what's missing in your own.

The air husband no. 2 took with him when he went away.

The money she never got from husband no. 3.

The butter dish husband no. 1 threw against the wall on the 10th of February 1972.

The woman returns with a twenty folded into quarters.

—You don't have to ask for jam jars, she says.

—They're for my bees, June says, taking the money.

In all ways, except the having of two beehives, June Wylie has nothing much to show for her life. But now, when all she wanted was a few jam jars, she is twenty euro up.

—You keep bees? Where?

—In hives, June says.

—Hives, where?

—At my house, June says. And I always need jars.

3

—Is it the season?

It's the season, sure enough. Plenty of flowers, a nice bit of rain, the bee populace keen for work. But June knows what the woman is getting at. No one with that accent has the land for hives.

—Are you nearby? Tessa says. I'm Tessa by the way.

—In the terrace behind the national school, June says.

—I'll have to take a walk past.

—Just to check that I have the bees?

It takes one to know one, and this Tessa one lives here alone. Those flowers are too simple to have been bought by anyone else. And that make-up is for her own amusement. Who gets a hairdo and puts on yoga pants? But June doesn't think Tessa always lived here like this. A view of the sea is not something you ever plan on stomaching alone.

—You're a fascinating creature, Tessa says. Who are you? Tell me.

How do you begin to describe yourself; how can you describe a person? June has bees but she's not a beekeeper, she doesn't know other people who have bees, you're not going to see her at any fêtes.

She's not the type of woman you'd look twice at. Once upon a time she had herself down for Chrissie Hynde, but punks get old, and some punks can't afford the upkeep, and some punks can't be arsed with it. June put it down to the hairdressers being closed since Covid, but the hairdressers are back open a good while now.

June cleans houses; there are bleach burns up her arms, the elastic is gone in her trousers. It's her eyesight, it's her bones, she has a new hip, she has two of them.

4

She's from the old days, when things were better, and they weren't as good.

She smokes, she has bad breath, she sleeps in, she's been told she's hard, and she is hard, and she's so soft that she cries at cartoons seen through someone's living room window.

She's the grass that needs cut. She's yesterday's eyeliner today. She's the skirt tucked into tights, the phone number with the digit left off. She's margarine, tap water and a packed lunch, she's a bad mattress, she is borrowed Wi-Fi, she is black nights.

She can't even say who she is, she's nothing to speak of.

Tessa says she has something in the oven, and even high protein diets don't recommend an entire chicken for lunch. Would June like to join her?

Bingo.

June is rarely wrong, and she is as nice as can be in circumstances that involve terror at giving or receiving invitations.

There are chicken smells and there are chicken smells, and this is very chickeny, but June says thanks for the money, and no thanks to the meal. The last time she went anywhere for dinner, she was so nervous that she wet herself in her neighbour's porch. But there's no point in ignoring the fact that she spends her life crying out for company.

Her life is spent polishing floors in other peoples' houses, filling and emptying buckets, taking out the bins, cleaning out the bins before running for a bus to another house—with no one ever home—to do the exact same routine, always out or back in the dark, all to allow her to travel undetected and alone. June Wylie is long past needing to leave any trace in the world.

She'll walk a half-length of the pier before turning up for home. Later there'll be a packet of soup and toast from the end of loaf and in the morning, there'll be honey.

Tessa will figure out something to do with the leftovers, and who knows if she'll receive any other unexpected visitors? June knows what it's like to wish too much for things, for someone to go upstairs to, an occasion to get dressed up for, a dinner that you didn't cook, afterwards a thank you letter to come in the door saying everything except what you want it to.

Another life is still possible.

Ray Draper falls in love six times a day.

He's heading down Tivoli Road, and he's fallen in love with the person in the Micra. Her face and all her thoughts. He wants to change direction and cycle along with her.

Someone else on a racer, balancing a coffee and a bag of books. That's two.

There is a peacock going mad in someone's garden.

He falls in love with the peacock.

He passes a cat asleep on a car bonnet.

In love with the cat.

When he sees a young African lad in a three-piece suit asleep on a bench outside the shopping centre, Ray doesn't have to convince himself that this person isn't worthy of someone.

Now there's the strong possibility of falling in love with the new receptionist at the doctor's surgery. There's a wholesomeness that might rub off on him.

Aileen's new. She doesn't seem to know how it works.

—Do you have an appointment? she says.

—This is more of a drop-in type situation, Ray says.

—We're out the door, she says. You need an appointment.

—I'm a regular, he says.

—We're overloaded with them, Aileen says.

—Isn't it great to be in such demand?

He doesn't want to be rude, but Ray is one of their best patients.

He settles in with a magazine by the window. The oul one beside him looks to be at her last station, but still she's showered and dressed up nicely and has been driven down here in search of some small tenderness.

Carla, the doctor, is that nice to anyone.

She passes through the reception with a look to Ray that says he'll be made part of the plan for the day. Aileen, the receptionist, is to stick him in over lunch. They'll talk while Carla has her sandwich.

Including Aileen and the oul one, that's three interactions from the one location, and all in the time it takes for Aileen to heat up some soup (she knocks off the phone and takes her food outside to the bench). Ray reckons he might even hit it off with her one day.

If Ray had known he liked people sooner, he would have talked to more of them earlier in life. He would not have been so choosy. Now, he'll talk to anyone.

If you're home from four and you're not out and about till ten the next morning, that's eighteen hours. You must really like your own company to be in it for a whole eighteen hours. But there's people to see at the tennis courts, down on the pier, here at the doctors. The circuit might happen two or three or four times in a day and, those days, when he's on a roll, Ray will talk to anyone about absolutely anything.

He'll talk about the weather, how it's been, how it's going to be, the impact that'll have on the match, the garden, traffic, everyone.

He can talk about church roofs, astroturf, the afterlife, tech booms, Holy Roman Empires, fish farms, Coco Gauff, terrorism, gossip, gospel, and any ailment you like, especially low blood pressure, fallen arches, and arthritis, and if you'd like to hear about the desperate state of Ray's knees, he'd gladly converse with you about his knees.

Carla's tired. Working too hard, caring too much.

Too many Rays, Ray thinks.

You make many friends in life, if you know how to go about that kind of thing. The friendship with the woman who checks your blood for beasties and sticks their finger up your you-know-what is only as important as any other.

Everyone's after the same thing. Someone to bind you to the place.

And Ray is good friends with Carla.

She brings him bags of her muesli mix.

She's a member of the tennis club in Sandycove, but she makes a point of playing up at public courts on the days that he's working.

She gets her kids to sign his Christmas cards.

She offered him the code for her Spotify so Ray could find some of the old soul stuff (he wanted to play her some Curtis Mayfield), but he lost the bit of paper she wrote it on and was too shy to ask for another.

—How've you been? Carla asks.

If it's one of those questions that you either like or don't like, today Ray quite likes it. He warmed himself up for the cycle with a bit of the dancing Carla has recommended.

It's a kind of a yoga thing, the dancing, you're moving—no, you're grooving—and you're doing yourself good.

Ten minutes usually does him. The moves are everyday actions, lightly modified.

Scrambling eggs in a hurry.

Head stuck in a lampshade.

Hoovering the walls.

Losing the scissors.

Bad at the cello.

Sewing on a slippery button.

Indecisive barbecuing.

Hammering a nail with your elbows.

It usually takes four or five goes of '96 Tears'—an open invitation to some very nice moves —and a quick belt of 'Louie Louie' to get him out the door.

Ray Draper is not the type of man you'd look twice at, except for the fact he seems to want you to. But the bandana on the forehead is for practical reasons: Ray cycles a lot (it's easier on the knees), and he sweats a lot.

Everyone calls the tennis gear eccentric, but it can't be eccentric if the clothes are yours and they fit. The t-shirts are made from good cloth, they've another thousand washes in them.

People ask him about the Discman and all Ray says is that it's never given him any trouble. He needs his tunes on his cycles. Roberta Flack's version of 'Bridge Over Troubled Water' only comes into its own after the thirty-fifth listen. It stops being music. You become it and it becomes you.

—Have we anything to worry about? Carla says.

—Do you never get tired of talking to sick people?

—Some of them leave a little better, Carla says.

—A little go of the magic sponge. What about yer one who was dressed up to go the races?

—She's not much older than you, Ray. And maybe you'd want to be a little less pass-remarkable.

He appreciates the direct approach, or if it's a form of indirection, Ray appreciates that too. Life is best seen as a riddle. The real question being, Ray, what's wrong with you now that wasn't a problem a week ago?

Do we have to take another go at your colon?

Has it ever occurred to you to even look at a tin of peas?

I'm building up to peas, is what Ray might say.

In return Carla might tell him that vegetables do indeed take a bit of building up to.

—I'll have to keep going here, she says.

—Check-up complete? Ray says.

—I'll file the paperwork.

—Fit as a fiddle?

—Easy now, she says.

Once you're in you're in, so June drops home the jars and takes the full ones that she has left down to see her friend Preet.

Why does the Sari Grocery remind her of London? For all the deluxeness, Dublin is only catching up with the London June knew of 1989, or even 1976. It's not a proper city until you really hate it, and June had the qualifications to truly hate London and now she hates Dublin, not as much, but enough to acknowledge the fact that it's become a proper city, and one that she wants no part of.

At least there are more black people now, and brown and yellow people, most of whom pick up after other people like June and Preet do.

The Sari Grocery carries a lot of stock, and there are the best mangoes money can buy, plus some of the lesser mangoes, and smokers like clove toothpaste. June would have it for dessert. Preet serves home-cooking from a hatch in the back of the shop, where she keeps a display of June's honey on the counter with a hand-written note about the bees being from the neighbourhood; local bees carrying vague associations of affluence.

The facts: the fifty euro a month that June earns from the honey makes all the difference. Preet feeds her for nothing, but this is one of the few places that she can afford to eat in. The spicing can be vicious, but Preet always has something on the go that June can eat.

Today it's a nice mush of yellow lentils that doesn't care if you call it a soup or a stew.

—This is so nice, June says.

Preet goes back to *The Chandigarh Tribune*. She is seventy-five and only looks it because this kitchen and all the rooms in her life get scrubbed to within an inch of themselves. When they met, she was even quieter than she is now, and what Preet does ever say is in a throaty voice that communicates a bewilderment and excitement the rest of her works to belie.

June keeps talking to her food.

—This'd make you weep, she says, and without looking up from the paper, Preet ladles a little more dahl into the bowl.

Preet would give everything in the shop away for free, but the Sari Grocery is owned by her nephew Gurjit who also has a restaurant which has nearly won a Michelin Star so many times that the experience has presented him with some kind of spiritual enlightenment. Even though Punjabis aren't big on rice most of the stuff consumed in south county Dublin comes in from the Sari Grocery. It comes in sacks the size of futons.

—Would you like something different tomorrow? Preet says.

—What is there? June says.

—I have some spinach.

There is always something that needs to be used up.

June returns the bowl, but Preet waves away the thank you. Then Gurjit walks into the room as though he's in search of a waiter to give out to.

Someone once gave this man the idea that short, tight, black suits and patent leather shoes looked good on a man of twenty-five stone.

She used to clean his house until he got one of his aunties to do it, and even now Gurjit regards June as someone who knows too much about what he does to the towels. If it wasn't for the fact that he flew all his aunts over from India in the first place, and that he sells only the oiliest cardamom and the reddest cloves, she would regard him as a fool in a boyband suit.

—I want the honey gone, he says.

Preet looks over at him but returns to the paper.

—What's it doing wrong? June says.

—It's confusing people.

—What's it doing?

—It's not Indian, Gurjit says.

When June was in the pubs, she was more alive to these kinds of things. Everyone has those days, you're stressed about the cost of the new extraction system, so you lash out at the person who stands all day at the cooker. Perhaps Gurjit's just paid the week's wages, gone through the invoices for light and heat and fuel, spoken to the accountant who's reminded him about fourteen new kinds of tax and all the levies for late payment.

Some old woman's honey is next on the list.

—You're always hanging around here, Gurjit says.

—I come for your auntie's food, June says.

—So do I but I don't hang around. It's not a nightclub.

Cleaners know how to make themselves small, and she says, —No, it isn't.

It's a shop selling coriander out of polystyrene boxes.

June doesn't point out to Gurjit that it is also a community centre, and without it she'd have nowhere to go. Sometimes she walks in here, and when Preet says hello, it is the first time someone has said something to June all week.

June knows to rely on her own devices, reliably superpowered by the right kind of mango, and assembling a living from multiple jobs and an incomplete state pension, so many ambitions in life, none of them realised, which is proof enough that she needs to take her honey elsewhere and this is all that she deserves for ever counting on anyone.

These are all the thoughts of a split-second.

The last time she cried was when Mik Bolger stole all the strawberry plants from her front garden. The Bolgers—first cousins to husband no. 1—don't tend to discriminate in choosing their targets, but they do seem to have it in for old women who keep bees. Mik Bolger is scared of bees and seems to know that if he takes it out on June, the bees won't know the difference.

This all happened the one time June invited Preet over for tea. They'd taken chairs from the kitchen and set a little table for themselves outside. There was a stool with a tray on it, teacups and sugar cubes and things. The milk even went in a jug.

The little bit of garden is the size of a box room, and June and Preet were nicely tucked in behind the hedge and the old rambling rose. The bees were in fine form, too, coming and going, and Preet wasn't fussed about them, she wasn't saying much at all. The only thing guaranteed to bring a smile to Preet's face is a European biscuit, and June was in and out to the kitchen for Bourbon Creams and Toffypops—Preet gave out an Indian granny whoop at the sight of a Jammie Dodger. Mik Bolger must have been there most of the afternoon waiting for his moment. The hives are tilted to prevent rainwater from pooling, and he came through the hedge at just the right angle to topple one into Preet's lap. The hive fell over, and though she knew to get herself out of there, Preet didn't want to move away without clearing up the cups, she was stacking saucers on top of plates, and it's approaching a miracle that she didn't get stung—June thinks the bees were confused—and, with Bolger singing out from behind the hedge about chocolate Labradors. He was singing 'Brown Girl in the Ring'.

It's no job for an old woman with hips and heart trouble, but June suited up and spent the entire night getting the hive upright. She woke up the next morning and the strawberries were gone. She found the plants thrown over a wall by the Eagle House, and the net in the bins by the bus stop. She cut the net into pieces and then June lit a fire in June to burn all the remnants.

Crying is supposed to make things better. With it all came the shame that everything else in life must measure up to.

It was like June was sobbing up the chimney.

She stayed in her pyjamas for days.

Preet's eating a cold roti, and so they don't have to talk about the honey anymore, Gurjit gives June a couple of twenties and a pat on the hand. Then he is onto a story about a soap star who keeps trying to order takeaway from the restaurant that doesn't do takeaway. He's going to drop her over a curry later, just to be funny.

Gurjit's funny stories are a sign for Preet to pack herself up if she wants a lift home. Is it quite clear that either June or the honey need someone to stand up for them?

June is waiting for Preet to say something in defence of a friend.

Preet would get up at four in the morning to wash the neighbour's windows, waiting until everyone was awake before starting up the mower to do the lawn, but it's too much, isn't it, to expect her to choose a friend over family?

One thing June knows not to do is ask too much of someone. But why does everyone keep giving her money?

Somewhere in this village there might be a pair of old people just like Ray and June.

Somewhere in this village there are old people nothing like them.

Somewhere in this village is a couple who've just met. Somewhere in this village is a couple who've just broken up.

Somewhere in this village is a person on an internet dating site. Somewhere in this village is a person without the internet, who is on their way out to a place where people gather. Somewhere in this village is a person who doesn't go out. Somewhere in this village is a person who will never go out again. Somewhere in this village is a person who would find that scenario sad, funny, or a relief.

Somewhere in this village is a person sweeping flies from a house before it's handed back to the bank. Somewhere in this village a person is cleaning up broken glass after a fight. Somewhere in this village a couple are making up after a fight. Somewhere in this village, a couple have broken up after a fight.

Somewhere in this village, a person is feeling misunderstood. Somewhere in this village a person is saying sorry. Somewhere in this village a person is saying sorry against their will. Somewhere in this village a person is saying sorry for the thousandth time.

Somewhere in this village is a person with no interest in love at all. Somewhere in this village is a person who has had theirs.

Somewhere in this village is a person poised for momentousness. Somewhere in this village is a person who doesn't know what momentousness is and will have no use for it if it ever presents itself.

Somewhere in this village is a caretaker.

Caretaker is a very nice word.

Care taker, care taking.

Ray is fine with any wording.

He's come to see himself as the guardian of the Clarinda Park tennis courts. He waits for the last game of the day to wrap up. People are punctual, people are polite, people are nice. It's easy to forget that. And Ray just needs to keep up the interactions.

One more good chat before turning in.

He cycles along the seafront but decides against the east pier. Last week, someone gave out to him for cycling on it.

Even before the knees went on him, Ray seldom walked anywhere. Here-to-there happens on two wheels.

It's a five speed Dawes, called after himself, not Ray but Raimund, meaning wise protector.

Ray would prefer it to mean light of the world.

Ray du monde, ray of light, anyway, Raimund is bonier than the bikes you see nowadays, and he's done Ray for forty years of freewheeling and being leaned on.

Something like 25,000 miles, the circumference of the earth, and if ever Ray's out of sorts, off he goes, cycling it away.

Nothing the matter with having a friend like that, and Raimund's never been off the road. One of the Bolgers from Eden Villas once set fire to him because he was locked to the railings outside the church.

There was war.

Ray cuts up through the town and considers a run through of the yellow stickers in M&S.

Or might have his tea out.

Chips or something that's not chips; sometimes he skips the evening meal altogether, and he'll get to bed feeling as empty as on old oil drum.

The echo in his belly now gives him a notion for spice. Turmeric is good for all sorts of different things—including the depression—but Ray has never had much spark with your one who does the cookery in the Sari Grocery. They reached the end of all the turmeric-based chat a long time ago.

Now he tends to be in and out. Five euro gets you

enough pakora to fill a bin bag. That's a fact worth celebrating.

Ray gets there just in time to see the owner fella sliding down the hatch on the kitchen. His auntie is sitting with her coat on at one of the high stools. Beside the auntie is a woman facing a load of sludge-coloured jam jars, moving them around like backgammon pieces.

It doesn't look like it's been the best of days. She starts putting the jars in her bag.

—Is there something the matter? Ray says.

—Why does there have to be something the matter?

—Just being nice. Can I ask what you're doing with those?

—The honey? It was for sale.

Ray is not going to get an invitation, but he waits a few moments before pulling up a stool. He's not really good with sad stuff, or real stuff, and it makes things harder, as she packs up the jars, to see this person working through what bad thing has happened to take her honey off the market.

And on the other side of the table, it is a mercy that June is beleaguered enough not to object to someone inviting themselves into her company. At their stage in life, one person can't just walk up to someone and open up to them. Is there time for any of that?

The polite part, the fun part, the silly part, the bad part, all in that order.

Ray knows how it works. Telepathy is guff. The horse who can predict the presidential elections. But he has wondered what it would be to present all your private thoughts to someone only to find there is no need to do so. The special feelings—grace, resignation, deep fulfilment—are already in place. And in that moment, it's true that Ray Draper and June Wylie are thinking and feeling the same thing.

It's all the nervousness that comes with making a new friend at any time in life.

June hopes she's not staring, and Ray hopes he's not staring.

She has a fine big forehead you could write a shopping list on. It's been out in the sun, and her skin's nice, there's a twilight shine to it.

He's unable to decide which bit of her face to look at next.

She could have her back to him, and he'd be fascinated by her.

Ray would be looking when he isn't looking.

And June wonders who has hair that long at his age and if it always looks as if he's just got out of the shower. He shuffled in here, but his arms and legs are thick with freckles and wiry enough to signal him as someone who knows to mind themselves. There's a smell of the outdoors to him—a bit of grazed knees—and he looks entirely mad in that jumble of old sports gear.

And that's the whole picture, an entire person in half a second.

You have no notion of a person's existence and then you do.

June looks to Ray—please, ask me not to go—and she heads for the door. Ray gets there before her.

—What are you going to do with them jars? he says.

Every thought seems to show on his face as it passes, and his eyes are quite hesitant, June thinks, that's nice, too.

—They're coming home with me, she says.

—Does that mean they're still for sale? Ray says.

—It depends.

—What if I offer to buy them?

Ray gives her a twenty for the jars and, after a quick cheerio to all concerned, sets off down the street, swinging the bag.

June steps outside to take another look. All she can see is this strange man with a bag filled with her honey, and all she can think about is this strange man, and how this might be the last she'll ever see of him.

He swings the bag so high that for a moment June thinks he's going to hurl it into mid-air.

2

The bee part of being the bee

When the weather is as good as this June likes to take her breakfast outside, and she is in her little garden soon after dawn.

There's nothing in the fridge—there hasn't been for weeks—so she settles on some black tea as she waters pots that don't really require it and sweeps the path and deals with the clippings from yesterday's blitz on the rambling rose.

The bees have caught on to the general can do-ness, busy-busy, but June hasn't got much into the pots this year and whatever is up and ready for pulling (a few lettuces that aren't going to reach much of a peak), she will drop into the grocery for Preet. They can't leave things as they did yesterday.

She smokes three rollies a day, in a breakfast, lunch and dinner arrangement. After breakfast, hoping to have avoided the morning rush, June heads down for a swim.

The Forty Foot is the reason why most people come here, but June doesn't swim there anymore. All that jollity, all that vitality, which is the jollity and vitality of having enough time and money to transform yourself into something as worthwhile as a fruit bowl.

The people at the cove around the corner are that bit more sound, and while she's not one for the chats, June goes along with it because people in their togs are the friendliest they'll ever be—padding around like they're all crowded into the bathroom at home.

People forget where they are.

There are bodies and there are bodies, and June's seen more complicated vein situations than she ever thought she would.

The state of people.

The state of her.

She slips into the water, a buffalo entering a watering hole.

The bay is extortionate-looking, solid blue, and the thing about the sea in June is that it's had just a little of summer to heat up but there's still a good shock in it. The air is digestive, there's nourishment from the water, and the waves have a gentleness she hasn't felt in a while.

Husband no. 2 used to swim in the sea as much June did, but he was Italian, and she was better at being in the cold than he was.

Why do I always want to go the toilet? he'd say.

Belt away, she'd say.

I might do, he'd say.

How do you know I'm not pissing now? she'd say.

Are you? he'd say.

Might be, she'd say.

Really?

Might be.

And nice thoughts of husband no. 2—God love him—
are just a reminder of the possibility of having made a new
friend in Ray.

Last night as she got in, so exhausted from trying not to
cry in front of Gurjit and Preet that June started to undress
in the hall, she spoke to herself so forcefully that she heard
a voice coming back from the tiles. Let's hope this person
is good to you, it said.

A little daytime nap.

This is only to make up for the lack of nighttime naps.
Nighttime naps are few and far between at the moment.
With them come the sad dreams: Ray's heart is a roll of
old linoleum, his heart is a fouled-up sleeping bag found
in a deserted carpark.

Sad dream.

No, his heart is a spoonful of jam, his heart is a sweet
little plum, his heart is a lemon bonbon, it is the melty bit
on the inside of a chocolate pudding.

And he won't run into anyone here. His supervisor has
been and gone to the courts for the day, they have done
their supervising, and now the afternoon can continue as
it is supposed to, without any supervision.

The supervisor's been saying Ray might want to think
about his disposition.

You're nice Ray, she says, and some people like you, but

most normal people think you look like Vitas Gerulaitis after a heavy weekend, and if they don't say the words Vitas Gerulaitis, it's because no one apart from you is placing any value on going around the place like a 1970s tennis player.

Ray Draper's just turned seventy, working seven days and being paid for three, and someone from the corporation is talking to him about his disposition.

Ray wakes up just in time to see little Timbo arriving with his mother, Mercy.

Timbo used to come along to chase the balls that flew over the fence until one day Ray invited him inside. Timbo and Mercy are not really tennis people, but Ray is not really tennis people.

Mercy has the basket of balls Ray lent them, and Timbo starts serving over and over into the same corner. Ray is sweating just looking at him, but sometimes, when some of the proper players aren't around, he and Timbo hit together. There's something exciting about getting your arse kicked by a twelve-year-old.

Ray is on his way down to the court when he remembers. The racquet Timbo's been playing with looks like it's been made from old toothbrushes. But a bit of asking around never does any harm, and Ray has a surprise for them. When he told people who it was for, he could have raised enough money for three new tennis courts (and he'll have to come back to that idea).

He went to the place in Dún Laoghaire shopping centre and spent the guts of an afternoon talking to someone who kept on telling him he'd find what he wanted online.

But Ray wanted to hold it in his hands.

The right tool for the assignment.

He goes back to the hut for it, and now Ray's practically running towards Timbo with a tennis racquet that's based on the one Roger Federer used and is great for hitting the ball on the run or standing still, with a cup of tea in your other hand. It's great for hitting the ball hard or soft. It's just great for hitting the ball.

Mercy's face is full of questions.

Who are you and what do you want?

It's not anger but when she places the racquet firmly back into Ray's hands, Mercy does look helpless.

There's no point in forcing kindness on someone. Ray leaves the racquet down and, like a child on litter duty, goes around the court collecting the tennis balls while Timbo lets rip with another load of serves that are fast and vicious enough to cause injury but are something to behold in the lines they draw. But the better Timbo serves, the more Ray wants him to try the new racquet. When one serve lands an inch or two long, Mercy shuffles over to inspect the gift. Ray can't understand what she is saying but from the boy's gestures, it has something to do with the way Timbo is throwing the ball.

Ray joins in with phrases that only sound convincing because he's heard them so many times out on the court.

Timbo's stance is fine, his toss is fine, but in the urge to move and keep moving, he's neglecting the positions.

The pose makes the action.

Arm up in the sky, coil yourself like you're a Greek statue.

Mercy is holding the new racquet out in front of her, before turning sideways to mime a shot that catches Timbo's eye. She asks him a question, but the boy gives no sense that he is interested or has heard a word.

He barely looks up when his mother hands him the racquet.

As easily as flicking a rubber band, Timbo makes the readjustment so that his left arm points to the sky, and the first five, ten, fifteen serves with the new racquet are identical and perfect and are fully deserving of all the applause and wolf-whistles from Ray.

But he's distracted by a silhouette at Timbo's end of the court.

It's not just a silhouette.

Ray's eyes are holding up well, and he can see her eyes, her nose, her scowl. That's a very lovely scowl.

He wonders if June's been summoned by his whistle.

Ray finds Timbo's old racquet and begins to hit, calling on all his moves, the stances he's picked up. June might fall for him for the footwork alone.

But he doesn't have the wrists for volleying.

They are thin wrists—womanly wrists, the family doctor once wrote. When everyone in school found out about that, they called him a queer, so Ray's father got him Indian clubs for strengthening exercises. So, he has the loose wrists, waggling the racquet and walking away from the line just before he makes a serve that Timbo clobbers back as if Ray has lobbed the ball in slo-mo.

June has stayed where she is. She has her eyes on them, and Ray hopes the frown is due to the sun. But someone else is striding in silhouette towards them. The small and sinister figure of Katrina McLoughlin has returned for some more supervision. Rather than take the path to the gate to the courts, Katrina crosses the grass to look through the fence at Timbo and his mother.

Mercy starts for the gate with her eyes to the ground, but Timbo is already through it, new racquet in hand.

There are some big trees, and Ray's seen him climb those before, but Ray catches sight of Timbo vaulting the bonnet of a moving car. Ray squeezes his eyes shut and when he opens them Timbo is making pace at the top of the hill, leaving him to begin the job of reasoning with Katrina.

She walks onto the court and, as the two of them begin silently collecting the balls, almost in anguish Ray sees that June has gone.

He barely hears Katrina when she says, —Haven't we talked about this?

—That it's a public tennis court?

—That people need to pay to be on.

—The courts weren't booked for that hour, Ray says.

—You need to pay if you're on them. And there are concessions for families in benefits.

—It's on me, Ray says.

—It's always on you, Ray, and I never see any money in that till.

Ray has his interactions—today has been good, today there have been seven—and Katrina must need her things, too.

She has new teeth (old teeth with a new front on them),

new nails (old nails with a new front on them), and a new car (completely new), and in all the bettering herself, she is very keen on a better Ireland, which sounds like the old Ireland that Ray can remember, and she can't, and what was better about it, anyway?

Ray lets her talk.

It's not his place to offer people free use of the facilities.

It's not his place to be deciding who gets charity and who doesn't.

Plus, Katrina's heard about the whip-round for Timbo's racquet and it's not Ray's place to be bothering people for handouts.

When she asks if he'd invite these people home, if he'd let them have a free for all with his own belongings, Ray decides not to share the fact he has already invited these people home, and they wouldn't come.

Until he reached the top of the housing list, he was far too familiar with couches and sleeping in peoples' attics. Ray was on the list for years, but his first words when he walked into his little flat just before last Christmas was— this'll do (a bathroom with no one else in it), and this'll do (the new bed), and so will this (the new mattress on the bed). He'd never had one of those before. He was petrified he'd do something to ruin it.

—I'd let you play, Ray says. If you were in any bother.

—That's nice of you, Katrina says. And if you did that, I'd report you.

Ray is very attached to his daydreams. Dreams are part of life. Sometimes they overflow into life, growing just as certain as anything that happens in a morning or a year a very long time ago.

The love part of love—the being in love with someone who's in love with you—is just something he's never got around to. Despite the fact Ray Draper likes women, and women seem to like him, they've never got on in that way, or got it on, which means doing it, which he's never really done.

You're a lovely man, do you know that? Hear that enough and anyone would get put off, and he got put off. But if Ray is going to go out of this world alone (all alone and getting aloner), then okay.

He did think he was in love, once.

Miranda, an Australian Miranda.

Neither of them had intended to end up there—she was to be inter-railing; he was to be on the sites in London—and they were both a bit embarrassed to have ended up in a shared caravan in the carpark behind a pub in Wexford Town.

The job was to pick the fruit on the farm.

The raspberries from her basket tasted better than his and Ray ate so much that it brought him out in hives. But it was hot under those nets, and when they were done at the end of the day, Ray and Miranda would hose off and eat out of the way of everyone else. The fields were all these mad colours, and the ground smelled like they did. Fruit, fermenting grass. They were going a few months and, one weekend, they went to stay in a little cottage in Wicklow. It was an Australian's idea of Ireland. And Miranda got what she wanted, the mist, the woodsmoke, icicles hanging from the gutters, frozen cobwebs, it was like Ray had laid it all on.

He was planning on asking her to marry him, and he was about to come out with it, and she knew he was going to, the poor thing, and the look in her eyes said she was going to say no. They were a million miles away from it.

Where did he go in that moment? Where does he go now?

Another version of the dream is that last night Ray bought some honey just to bring a smile to a stranger's face.

But he is not sure if this person wants a friend or even if he is good friend material.

He is so caught up in the dream that he does not register the fact that it is standing right in front of him. June has been there all this time, watching Ray and Katrina from a bench in the park.

—I'd like to say thanks for buying the honey, she says.

The noise in Ray's head is like the rush of a dual carriageway. He says, —I don't really like honey.

—Now you have six jars of it, June says. Can I buy you a drink to say thanks?

—I don't really drink, Ray says.

—It doesn't have to be drink-drink. It can be tea.

And Ray recovers his composure enough to say, —I could save us a walk, there's tea here. In my hut.

—Very seductive, June says. In your hut.

The sun has passed around to the hut's only window and, even with the windows open, the air is as thick as breath.

The afternoon is offering them its approval.

There is a moment where they both stare at a dog-bowl that for the life of him Ray can't remember where it came from. The first thing June does is get to work filling it up. Why there's no water in the bowl is beyond her.

—Where's the dog? she says.

—It's in case one shows up.

She takes Ray in again: the colour of him, the cut of him. Every now and again June's thought of getting herself a rescue dog—already she is coming to think of Ray as a nice dog she once knew. Cheerful and always pleased to see you, picking up sticks, and running through muck and leaving it after him.

—I thought that when we met, she says.

—Thought what? he says.

—You did remind me of a spaniel.

—I've never met a bad spaniel, he says. What kind?

—A wet one. Rust coloured, maybe.

—A little bit grizzled, Ray says.

—Wise, she says.

But look at how Ray is in his little hut, his way with a kettle. It takes him an age to line up all the boxes of tea on the table. Each one has tasting notes written in a childish hand.

—I like mine with honey, she says.

—I took it home, Ray says.

—But you don't like it?

—I'll bring it back in. Give it to people.

—I bet that little tennis fella likes honey.

—Did you see us? Ray says.

—You were lovely with him, June says.

—I feel like his great grandad.

—Do you? she says.

—Grandkids? he says. No, no kids to start with.

She shouldn't have asked him, that means he'll ask her. No, he doesn't, and June has no business going into any of that now. It's more that she has forgotten the thrill of watching someone else do something as simple and lovely as pouring hot water into a cup.

It is hardly a reason to be friends with someone, but—as Ray is finishing the tea, still wondering aloud about the dog-bowl—for June, in terms of perfect scenarios, this is near enough it. The delight Ray takes in warming the cups and letting everything infuse for exactly the time it says on the box.

His hands are quite something.

Paws.

Play-Doh fingers, but with slender wrists, floppy almost.

Imagine those, well, imagine those.

—It amazes me how much you like to follow instructions, she says.

—It amazes me too.

She notices a birthday card on the windowsill, just the one. A low-key operator.

Birthdays have come to be the most obvious sign of being alone. You get a reminder about your cervix from the doctor's (they'll stop, too, next year, when she's seventy-five) and you get a birthday card from the shop where you bought a bathmat you can't remember when.

—I don't want to burst your bubble, she says. But I

think I'm the older woman here. What did you do to celebrate your birthday?

—I came in here, Ray says.

—I'd rather you said you went for a check-up at the doctor's.

—I did that, too, he says.

—My birthdays are usually about as much craic as a phone call about your electricity bill. Last year I went for a walk to the big Dunnes in Cornelscourt.

—Long enough walk. Bet you took a taxi home?

—Taxi home is right, she says.

—We should go for a walk sometime, Ray says. I'll have to cycle beside you, but I can go very slowly. I could cycle you home now, I could meet the bees.

—They're not very interested in people, June says.

—Maybe I could apologise for not being gone on honey.

—They won't want to know, she says.

There is a rightness to the fact that June and Ray have lived here all their lives and have never met. Have they met before? Who knows? They might have run into each one of the days.

They aren't exactly intrepid, either of them, so it would have been in Dalkey, McDonagh's, when it was them that had it. Going quietly and relaxedly about their business kind of thing. June might have been the one skulking away from a hen she hadn't wanted to go to in the first place. Ray might have been the one with his arm in a sling, singing Amhrán na bhFiann into the dregs of a pint of Smithwick's.

The moments amalgamate into nothing.

No, they can't remember each other.

They don't press it, but it is a worry, the memory, or a blessing. And neither of them can understand how this village ended up being somewhere people move to.

There's the bay and the echo of a pair of hills, and it's the out-of-the-way feeling that people pay for, and that Ray and June have always depended on, and which now they wonder about. They don't talk much, except for Ray to say, —It's been great lately. Do you think we're in for one of those summers?

—Do *you* think we're in for one of those summers? June says.

But they are not going to let a little shyness get the better of them; it's that sweetness that they've craving all this time, for years the pair of them.

It could be that the sun has gone in, but June's garden is a bit grim. Ray is not going to say that the beehives resemble a pair of tower blocks before which everything else must make way; he is beset by ideas to spruce the place up.

He remembers what it felt like last night in the Sari Grocery. He had the urge to help someone who probably doesn't need any, and never has. But that impulse is joined by another one: if Ray doesn't offer June help, he may have no reason to be around.

He tries to keep himself from leaning on the beehives, and June, who's fussing around authoritatively with a bush, gives him a smile that makes him feel happy to be here and, now that he has been here and now that he has met the bees, wary of stepping out of line.

The flat once belonged to husband no. 1, who kept a motorbike in the little bit of garden, and the ground has a long a history of Castrol GTX and brake fluid dripping onto it. The paving slabs were placed directly onto the turf.

She starts singing a song: The worms crawl in and the worms crawl out, they crawl all over your chin and mouth.

It's a song from back then.

Of all the songs you could and couldn't sing.

It's been quite confusing being a Prod down here. When they've finished fucking the Queen, you can get on with fucking the pope, and best to be doing that up to your neck in Fenian blood. Her one ambition growing up near Belfast was not to live there and to forget that she was from there.

Husband no. 1 was Glasthule's first punk, taking to it because he was rough enough for it. He was everything June, at first, understood punk to be. She was planning on running out on him and then his luck did.

Dead by stabbing about fifty feet from here.

A broken bottle, which was a bit harsh when you think about how fastidious he was about flick-knives. But that was the life he led. He was a walking split lip.

This was fifty years ago.

But last week June was fourteen years old, being expelled from school for refusing to sing in church.

Two weeks ago, she was twenty.

Two weeks ago, she was thirty, and forty and fifty and sixty.

She can't imagine what age she will be tomorrow.

—That's you met the bees then, she says.

—Charming bunch of lads, Ray says. Do you really think they don't mind if I don't like honey?

—They don't expect anyone to like them.

Then Ray catches June's eye, and it occurs to him that they haven't really done that yet: exist for one another simultaneously, Ray in June's mind and her in his.

That's how it feels to her, too.

You meet someone and from that moment on you don't want to be away from them. But they aren't to know. Perhaps they don't think that it will ever amount to anything.

How much honey can two hives make? Ray wonders. But June's as well trying to figure out what it's like for the bee to be the bee. They are there for a while talking about the hives.

Bees chatting, bees in the huff, bees being narky, bees doing it, bees not doing it.

And parasites and viruses, and the perils of seeing the insects through a winter, none of which Ray listens to as he's trying to see what's through the living room window.

A couch and two chairs and a telly.

What could be more lovely than to sit there and be brought something on a tray. A curry makes sense, with all the windows steamed up from the cooking of the rice. He never makes rice when it's just himself.

Now that he has stopped fidgeting, they are both being very still, too still, and June thinks Ray's doing too much breathing. In and out, too slowly, and so audibly that she can imagine him breathing his last.

—I think that'll be us for tonight, she says.

There are many reasons why Ray is not being invited in.

1) She's tired and she wants to put on a *Midsomer Murders*.

2) And who is Ray anyway? Some nice man who talks too much.

3) The last person June invited told her the place smelled of old carpet.

4) She's not ready for someone to die on her.

3

Goodbye picnic basket

Hello? Hello. Hello! Yes, June, it's Ray Draper. Your number's in the book, June Wylie, that's you, I think, so I'm calling to say thank you for thanking me for the other night, no harm in another thanks, I don't think. But I get the impression you're not big on people coming in your house, and I'm kind of the same, as in, it's never happened, so I was thinking of asking you out for a picnic. A picnic can cover all eventualities. You can eat as much or as little as you like. I'll do the food, there's this picnic-basket-rucksack thing that I got as a present. I've never had the occasion, but I think this could be it. You're on in the mornings, aren't you? What time do you finish? The afternoon doesn't look that good, but we can meet at four at Glasthule Dart station before walking around to work up an appetite for an early grub at the bandstand on the pier. Okay, June, all the best.

All the best?

Ray is being too pleasant by half, and it is pleasantries that drive June Wylie mad. What a performance leisure has become. People used to go straight home after work.

They used to wait in for the news, they used to be affected by it.

Now there's suffering, so much of it, apocalypses and extinctions that don't seem to matter. It has to hurt, and none of it hurts anymore, and the disinfected milk costs fifty euro, and June has been invited out for a picnic, and she has become very, very cranky.

Ray doesn't leave a number either.

Either she must go when he says she's to go or she won't turn up at all.

The day isn't doing what it's supposed to do. The sky is virtually black, and Ray doesn't know whether to suggest eating indoors or be an eejit and drag a picnic to the pier in a screaming wind.

He takes out the wicker rucksack that was a donation from one of the former residents in the square. But he hasn't made food for anyone in a very, very long time and the sandwiches you have at home don't seem good when you take them out of a bag in public.

He goes to the village and spends a wicked amount on a few crackers and a small tub of mackerel pâté.

He's brought other things from home, soup in a flask—there's no life without soup—and he wanders along just before the appointed time, approaching the station just as Johnny Mulholland is barrelling out of it on his way down to the village.

Johnny was captain of this that and the other at school (class of 1972). There was, then, a right way and a wrong way for young men to go about their business. Pints, woolly jumpers, Thin Lizzy.

When Ray went off to take a stab at university (disastrous, short), Johnny cruised towards being a consultant anaesthetist in Minneapolis, Zürich, and then at St Vincent's in Dublin where he became the person that they wheel out to talk about waiting lists on the Sunday morning radio shows. Ray hears Johnny's voice so often that they may as well be in regular contact. It could be a few weeks since they've met, or twenty or thirty years, but it's more like fifty.

Conversations tend to go at Johnny's pace and, once he's delivered the news that he's off for the few in Fitzies, he's taking a moment or two to size Ray up.

It's likely that meeting Ray will plunge the graph of Johnny's day a little. He wants to get on with his pints, but he can't leave without saying, —We didn't hear much about you, Ray. It was architecture at one point, wasn't it?

—And a bit of loafing about. Tree surgery.

—And you turned that into an occupation?

—Flat out, Ray says.

—You haven't changed, Johnny says. But you look like you've been away.

Johnny is used to people reporting to him and he is waiting for Ray to say more.

Nobody ever asks but everyone wants to know about the year, give or take, that Raymond Draper spent in the

43

abbey, the year it took to not become a monk. And what does everyone want to know anyway?

Spill the beans, they say. What did God have to say for himself, then?

As far as Ray was concerned, he's never set foot in any monastery. The older you get, the worse your memory becomes, and not everyone will have a past, anyway. If you don't remember something it doesn't exist, and it would be strange to think about something that doesn't exist.

They stand together at the door to the Dart station in the same way as they would if Ray accepted Johnny's invitation for the three or four pints (on him), companionably, but with nothing to say for themselves that the other person would have any use for.

—Are you sure you won't come down for the one? Johnny says.

Ray makes out that he's giving it a moment's reflection.

Today it has been necessary to spend seventy-five euro in a delicatessen and still wonder if he's bought anything to eat.

Ray's only thought when he sees June in the lane by the station is that he's five minutes late, and that he's had that time with her stolen from him.

—Busy morning? Ray says.

—I was in Foxrock polishing silver, she says. Quite therapeutic.

But June has a few questions. If she has thanked Ray for buying the honey, she doesn't need thanked back.

This friendship needn't be series of transactions, that's the first thing.

—What do you want out of this situation? she says.

—I didn't know it was one of those, Ray says.

—A picnic counts as a situation. And I'm working all day, I might have plans in the afternoon. I might be tired. Don't you get tired?

—That's one thing you can be sure of, Ray says.

—An afternoon out wasn't really what I wanted, June says. But I don't want you to be embarrassed either. I don't think you are easy to embarrass.

—No, I am, Ray says.

—I don't like to be sent instructions. I like to be asked what I think. And, unless you own a house in Killiney, and you want me to clean it, I'm unlikely to come when you say so.

Ray hadn't planned to be starting off with an apology, but June's serious, and she wants to be listened to.

—So what do we do? Ray says.

—That's better, she says. What do you think?

—What do *you* think? he says. I was thinking we might chance a picnic.

—Lovely idea, June says. Where?

—The bandstand at the pier. A bit of shelter from the elements.

—Lovely, she says. We'll be there in no time.

—But I haven't told you my itinerary yet, he says.

—No, she says. I don't like itineraries. We make plans together.

—Would you like to take a walk to the Forty Foot before we eat?

—That question suggests you have decided you want a swim.

—I've never been a swimmer, Ray says.

—And you've never asked me if I am or not.

—Is that what I'm supposed to do now? he says.

—And we don't have to do the same things at the same time. I can swim if I want to, and you don't have to, if you don't want to.

—Do you have your togs with you?

—No.

—What'll we do then? he says.

—Let's take a walk to the Forty Foot before we eat.

—Lovely idea, Ray says.

They head along the esplanade that faces the bay. June did have it in mind that they'd head into town, but Ray doesn't like to go into town, he doesn't like to go north of Sydney Parade.

Why would he do that?

It's all here, he says.

Falling in love, all here.

Being a fool, it's all here.

Eternal life, it's not here but the path to it is.

The good life and the things you do to attain a good life, the mountains and the sea, if any of that is enough for you, it's all here and not here, too.

Going out walking, it's all here.

Going out walking in a kaftan, it's all here. Walking into the sea and not coming out again, it's all here.

Bleak winters and sweet summers, all here.

Collecting shells, it's all here.

Collecting Steinway pianos, it's all here.

Running up a hill, it's all here, walking down the hill, going for a pint with Johnny Mulholland, having another one, having ten pints, and waking up on a bench surrounded by schoolchildren, it's all here.

Neighbours, friends, long lost friends, sworn enemies and lovers, kindly strangers that you'd like to know, and the ones you'd like to avoid, they're all here.

Neighbourliness, it's all here. Antisocial behaviour, that's here too. Crime, murder, rape, abuse of every kind, it's all here. Justice, that's here, injustice, moral pragmatism, moral cynicism, immorality, amorality, it's all here. Faith and God and religion, it's all here.

Staying true to who you are, it's all here. Becoming who you are, it's all here. Reinventing yourself, it's all here.

Colonoscopies, reiki, acupuncture, chiropody, psychotherapy, cancer scares, cancer, Botox, it's all here. Capitalism, liberalism, charity, activism and apathy, it's all here. Fascism, racism, it's all here.

The spirit world, it's all here. Sustenance and hope, it's all here.

Getting serious, getting off, getting real, it's all here.

Being there, it's all here. Why would Ray ever leave?

It's a strange habit, but Ray likes to remove his shoes to get the best out of a walk. The ground is wet underfoot but the grass is every colour of green—there are spring and summer greens, and there are winter and autumn greens, and they are all here—and he wants to take them all in and talk to June about them.

But June wants to sit on a bench, and Ray says to keep going. He's not sure how long the flask will keep the soup hot for, and he doesn't want the food that's supposed to be eaten hot to get cold, and once he is on his way somewhere he never wants to stop.

They really have to work at this, she thinks.

There's a nice little spot by the old diving club. People tend to pass it by on their way to the Forty Foot and they might have it to themselves. June suggests they have the soup now and the sandwiches in a bit, a radical move Ray is the first to agree.

—I was really thinking we'd have the cold stuff before the hot stuff, he says. I've got cheese and spread. All manner of other bits and pieces.

He's fallen into a terrible hole.

Johnny will be on his second pint by now, and Ray will be as distinguishable to him as a face on the Dart. If Ray had said anymore to Johnny, he might have been told that he'd squandered his good start in life.

Survival has been Ray's success.

But they find a little spot at June's suggestion and Ray begins delving into his wicker contraption and coming up with ramekins and saucers and tiny forks and spoons June can't have imagined him owning, or anyone finding a use for. The soup part of the picnic consists of perfectly stacked items existing in a lovely state somewhere between food and plaything. The flask is so sleek that it belongs in a pharmacy.

Even the pouring of the soup is an undertaking. Abracadabra it gets transferred to little stainless steel mugs.

—Do we need all the gizmos? June says.

—We do, Ray says solemnly.

—But it's a lovely arrangement. Do you get much use out of it?

—First time, Ray says. But I practised at home first.

They have the soup—minestrone something; June doesn't like it but doesn't say so—and once Ray has rinsed out all the cups and saucers in the sea, they continue the walk.

There is a crowd gathered at the Forty Foot, a charity swim of some kind. Swimmers crowd along the path and slip into the water with curses.

June and Ray stand near the rock that serves as a diving-board. The water is fizzing with pink, angry bodies. The other spectators, flattened into silhouette by the sun, look like mourners at a graveside.

It is an ordinary afternoon, and no one would notice Ray or June or care if they slipped away, especially now that the swimmers have reached the expanse of the bay, and the water has returned to a simmer.

It begins to lash rain but, rather than trot the short journey home, June suggests they take shelter under the canopy the swimmers use to change under.

The sugary stone is damp but everything else is gleaming from the soaking and some unexpected sunshine.

But they've been talking for a good while and Ray feels they have hardly revealed anything of themselves. First of all, to fully understand the path Ray Draper's taken in life would be to assume strange things of him. He's been a lollipop man, he's been a landscape gardener, he's been a Samaritan (not a very good one), he's been a barman, a bin man.

If there's a job to be had in south county Dublin with shite pay, you can count on him to have done it.

As if Ray's still answering Johnny Mulholland's question, he begins to tell June what happened when he left school in the early seventies.

—I had a few good years of thinking I'd be a painter when I grew up. Not houses, oils. But then I kept finding myself drawing pictures of houses. Square box. Chimney. Smoke. Sky. It was very calming, but this was a plan without much going for it. An expensive education and I didn't have the points to get into arts let alone architecture. But they let me enrol in a foundation course and I gave myself to it completely. But my nervousness at any space I might design became so much a part of my way of doing it, that I began to get things wrong on purpose. If I drew one staircase too many, I would make a case for keeping it in later. Doorways to nowhere, blocked off windows, I'd call an accidental cupboard the good room. You might even admire the pleasure I took in the oddities; I became known in my class for them. The mistakes were more remarkable than any clean line or hidden storage. There was a stubbornness to it that I find weird to talk about. I'm not like that now.

—You don't seem too stubborn, June says. Quite stubborn, though.

There is always weight to her words, a voice you could

sleep under. Like cream on the Irish coffee. He's tried saying it to her, but there's still no place for compliments.

Sour cream, maybe.

—Most of it's been bet out of me, he says. But this was a long time ago. It wasn't just a question of where people would live but how they would live, meaning that I wanted to go back to the beginning. After I got on my feet as an architect, I'd make enough money for a site on an island, Achill or somewhere. And there was something beautiful about a house built entirely from Irish spruce. All columns, pillars, beams, struts, stairs, floors, bannisters, all of it. Irish trees are Irish trees, and I didn't want to hear another word about the poor curlews who were getting put out of them. It'll look like a sauna, they said, a shed, but I got hold of some samples, and the wood in the model I made turned the colour it was supposed to, the yellowing was completely normal, and I wouldn't paint it for them. By the time they gave me my marks, I knew to the letter what it was called. I had a spent a very long time designing a piss-house. I think they still talk about it in the college.

That was it for Raymond Draper and architecture, he was a few years at the tree surgery after that. Not to mention the year in the abbey, which he never mentions.

Ray's waiting for June to reciprocate, but as far as she's concerned, you can know too much about someone. The more you know the more there is to dislike. In-depth isn't always best (except when you're doing an oven) and June Wylie doesn't want anyone inspecting her soul for flaws.

*

51

It's just them on this walk, there's no debating it. And June wants to share, she wants to talk, so she tries. But they have both forgotten half the things they've done, and June shares a story about a brawl at her first wedding that actually took place in three different times and three different places.

There's a real kick in amnesia, they both agree.

—It's not that we forget, Ray says.

—What then?

—We just outlast our memories.

—You're good, she says. What else is there to eat?

—I forget, he says.

June's worried that Ray spent too much on the picnic. He says that he hasn't.

Life has gotten very complicated, and life is very simple. It's your own fault if you're poor. This they know, and there's one solution: everyone is the same naked. The Forty Foot still has its share of old men going commando and it's impossible not to find old men in the nude very uninteresting but hilarious. They could be crawling from a shipwreck.

And it'll make a fun view for a picnic.

It seems like a good idea to lug the picnic basket up to the Forty Foot's top rock. Ray helps June then clambers up to put out the cheese and the ham and the rolls. He's got the message now, and there's less faffing around with making the sandwiches.

It is all lovely for a minute or two.

June has an eye for all the nice fixings that cost Ray all that money. It is always a question of money; neither of them has enough of it, he comes from it, and June's had it, and neither of them do now, and it's weird how much of life depends on it, and nothing does.

June pulls a face when the mackerel pâté appears, so it gets fucked into the sea. But now they are both, with elbows out, preparing sandwiches for themselves, and nodding along about the way ham was in the old days, carved from the bone by a butcher with bushy eyebrows and pencil in the pocket of his white coat.

In every way, this has been a funny little afternoon.

The person Ray wants so badly to make a connection with is eating the rolls he defrosted in his kitchen. But how can he be sure that having ham rolls isn't the height of it for them?

He can't be sure. Then, as if it has been casing the joint, a seagull walks very matter-of-factly across the rock and, with an insolent tilt of its head that Ray tries to reciprocate, starts to rummage around in all the packets. Manfully the gull begins choking down June's sandwich, flying up and off in a signal to others of its acquaintance to help themselves to more of the picnic, before all the birds pitch upwards as one, slices of cheese and ham held in the air like little flags.

The rest of the food slides from the rock into the water.

The wicker rucksack, too.

June takes Ray's hand to steady herself, but he's looking at his beloved picnic set floating in the sea, and not at her.

One irate swimmer starts gathering the bits of cheese and ham and flinging them onto the shore. Bad for the birds, he shouts.

The wind is kicking up again, and not content with ganging up on Ray and June, the seagulls are squabbling among themselves.

The swimmer ignores the calls to rescue the basket, which begins to bob off towards Wales, and the image sparks something in Ray. If he was as daring as he'd like June to believe, he'd be in the water to rescue it.

It is not the day he thought they'd have, but in the getting down from the top rock, which is a lot more difficult than the climbing up to it, they are reminded that this was all supposed to be fun.

Ray gets himself down first, managing to withstand the electric shocks in his ankles when he hits the ground, but in helping June down, he finds himself with her arse in his face and her hips in his hands. He was not counting on groping anyone today, and there isn't much in the fact of it being accidental.

He deposits her squarely onto the ground and raises his arms as if to say—here I am, there you are!

The rucksack is long gone, and the swimmer has left a pile of wet greaseproof paper at their feet.

When Ray bends down—knees!—to collect it, he notices the slipperiness of the light behind him, and he stays down there for a moment, looking up at her, daring June to know what he is thinking, and what all of a sudden has brought on these good spirits—being mugged by a seagull, being shouted at by a fat man in speedos.

They return to the shelter so Ray can find his tennis shoes.

—How long ago did we have the soup? June says.

—Dunno, Ray says.

—The rolls were nice, she says. But there wasn't much eating in them.

—I'll just have to give up on picnics.

—They don't suit us, June says. Eating cheese outside, it's not for the likes of you and me.

Ray was in junior infants with Emilio Minnelli, and sometimes, when he goes to the Savoy chipper, they let Ray have his food in the back where the staff have their breaks.

Emilio has long since retired to Puglia, but it's a family place and Ray likes to fit in with them by ordering his chips in Italian. Anita, Emilio's granddaughter, is learning Italian and they do a nice job of butchering the language with no one there to correct them. Ray has a phrasebook for the basics.

The phrase book is old, but languages are old. He'd like to understand what it feels like to be understood in another language. Do you get to understand more, and live more? You must do.

Una porzione abbondante di patate fritte, per favore.

Better words for things mean more feelings for things.

The little table by the window is free and Ray queues up while June decides between a batter burger or a sausage, one or two, two maybe, and it's no joke that Ray's eyes are feasting on her face, her nose, her cheeks, her mouth.

He can't be in love with just bits of her, with just her nose, or just her mouth, but he would be—she is a very symmetrical person—and if the parts make the whole, it's only because Ray prays that she will see past the scraps that he sees when he looks at himself.

They are people in pieces, and that's all Ray has for her. Bits.

Anita once let slip that the staff have pasta for their dinners, and Ray sometimes asks if there's any ragu on the go, and being out, and being out with June, has this effect on him now and he is getting excited, and the opportunity presents itself.

Ray orders and Anita asks him if they'd like to eat in the back, but June looks happy in the window and Ray goes over with the can of Coke she asked for and he is up to the counter again and back again and he is, tonight, incapable of seeing anything the matter with anything or anyone (and this will never change).

What will they talk about now?

Ray is never brighter than in his talk of the little Roma boy and the tennis, and how far he's come to get here at all, and how far he's come with the tennis, and how talented Timbo is.

Talent and discipline, all Timbo needs is a bit of good luck.

What a bright, beautiful picture Ray is painting.

Take another walk down there to see us, he says, fly your kite, soak it all in before I get fired for being too nice.

—Where will they go if they can't play there? June says.

Ray doesn't know the answer, and this isn't what's on her mind anyway.

If June makes the decision to invite Ray home now,

nothing silly is going to happen, they are both out the end of any of that, but once they have that out of the way, they might be able to enjoy wherever it is they will end up.

—And I've got something for you, Ray says.

—Why would you give me a gift? We've only met.

—It's in my pocket.

—You've been carrying it around with you?

—It's not big, he says.

He's stealing glances over to the counter, and June seems tired, they both do, and they're trying to pretend this has been the plan all along—throw the picnic basket into the sea and head to the Savoy—and when Anita calls out that their food is ready, Ray goes to get it.

He leaves the gift on the table—it's a bloody pebble—and he comes back from the counter, beaming.

—What's that? June says.

—It's slate, with a bit of quartz running through it. I thought it might like to live with the shells in your garden.

Ray has whole collections of these holy relics, he calls them. If he's cycling down the seafront, he's finding polished stones, it's fivers, it's perfectly good hairdryers, it's shoes and socks, who says they have to match? Things that the everyday folks leave behind.

He once found a Rolex watch on Dún Laoghaire pier, and handed it in.

—No, what's that? June says.

Anita has dropped off two big plates of pasta.

This is Minnelli's secret, assaulting you with such big portions that it will seem like everyone else is undergoing it, everyone else is doing you out of a proper dinner.

—Fettucine Bolognese, Ray says. It's what you get in Bologna. If you know you know.

—Where's my order? June says.

—I know them in here. This is what they eat. Do you not like a Bolognese?

—Not if I've just ordered a burger, no.

—Do you not like pasta?

—I was married to an Italian. But I like plain food. Spaghetti.

—On its own?

—Spaghetti on its own.

—No sauce? he says.

—No sauce, she says.

—No sauce on spaghetti?

—No.

—Spaghetti-spaghetti?

—Yes, she says.

—I could ask them to do some for you.

—Or you could get them to do me burger and chips, like I asked for.

She's gone quiet, June knows she's gone quiet. Ray gets her a burger, and now they have too much food they are not going to eat. She was brought up to admire stubbornness, and she does admire it, there is something in sticking to your guns, but June had two out of three husbands who were very principled about most things.

Ray hasn't a clue about people, and it's not her job to teach him. Once upon a time he might have been a project for someone, but June's too old for homework.

She's too old for being ordered for, she can choose her

own food, she's too old for a talking-to about what to put on your spaghetti, she's too old for those kinds of reminders.

She's too old for people who have to cycle to go for a walk.

She's too old for the Forty Foot, she's too old for seagulls, she's too old for cheese outdoors.

She's too old for people breathing while they eat, she's too old for parables about curlews in the spruce, she's too old for wooden piss-houses, she's too old for time bending on her, it might explode into memories she's absolutely no use for.

She is too old for acting like an old woman. She is too old for storming off.

Sandycove, and all its lavish goings-on. The water is creamy with its evening traffic, and that duel of hand-gliders has been put on just to supply something else for the eye-line.

God forbid the poor proportions of a thronged bay and an empty sky.

Tessa's door is open, there's a little drinks party on, and there is from everyone a sense of having done just enough, being born here, or taking the train for the evening, making millions or inheriting them, an all-round buoyancy that makes this the perfect village in which to pop into the neighbour's for drinks or to plot a hostile takeover in your swimming togs.

June takes a seat on the bench where they had their soup.

The pebble Ray gave her has been polished until it resembles porcelain. Pebbles are supposed to mean something, she supposes. It means that they're not really pebbles at all. It means he's sad, it means he's in need of some company, and it means he needs to do something to feel better about himself.

He is on the run from something, God help him, and so is she.

There's a young couple on their way down to the cove in dressing gowns. Swimming at night, it's the most intimate thing you can do without going all the way. If she does want to be friends with Ray, why does June want things to stay as they are? Even now, she wants the story to stay in the state of possibility.

Is this why Ray keeps on saying thank you, and giving her gifts? He doesn't have anything else that she might need.

And here he is now.

There are only so many paths someone can take on this seafront. The saunter is well practised, she decides, the saunter is very good as a matter of fact.

He joins June on the bench, and it's nice the way he has hands on his lap, the shapes they make, with the palms up, so she can take his hand if she wants to.

Ray lets June make the first move and she can tell from the way his hand feels in hers—soft and wrinkled, like dried fruit—that they will do their best for each other, but they will have to see how it goes. None of it has to be that bad.

—I'm tired, Ray.

—It's been a long day.

—Will you walk me home?

—I will, he says.

It's been a long day of talking, too, and the silence contains a resignation at everything not having gone quite to plan.

Ray gets June home, and he is about to let her go with a nice wave. If she were to speak, she'd say something like, sometime soon, I'm going to invite you in, but it won't be tonight.

She's rarely awake to see it get fully dark, and she doesn't go in straightaway. She hates going into a gloomy house, but there was no notion they'd be out this late.

The hives are big, dark blocks, staring out at anyone who might care to trespass on her little rectangle of land. In a million ways that June can't name, she feels lucky to have this place, and now that she's home she's not sure if she does ever want to invite anyone in. There are too many things to work out.

Just as Ray is nearly gone, to his picnics and his tennis, June calls after him, —Can I say something else?

—Go on, he says.

—All I'm saying is that I don't want anyone making my decisions for me.

—I understand, he says.

—But thank you for the stone, she says.

—I was waiting for the right moment.

—Don't you have someone else to give presents to?

—No, he says.

4

Think of what life'd be like
if I did everything you say

June went to bed before dark and had more sleep than was her share. She rescheduled her appointment at the doctor (the hips have settled in nicely) and the good fortune at missing another talking-to about the rollies has taken her through a morning of making herself look spick and span for her interview with Tessa. The best and most absurd part of this is that, as if by celestial intervention, on her way to the seafront, June passes her third husband lying on a single mattress at the door of Digby's restaurant on the seafront.

His cheeks are resting on the pavement.

June looks first at his chest, to ensure that he is breathing, and then at his face.

How could she be so thrilled at the sight of someone lying on the street, like a burst bin-bag, waiting for a lorry to back up and some men in hi-vis jackets to dispose of him?

Is it significant that he has collapsed by the restaurant where they chose to divorce?

Digby's was the kind of place where grown-ups went to get engaged or to have affairs (like she and husband no. 3 both ended up doing), the service circumspect but schooled enough to give you expectations that this happens everywhere; someone will be on hand in the morning to present the toast to you with tongs.

Only for her great capacity for dreaming sadness back into being, on any other day of the week, June has no issue with ignoring husband no. 3's continued existence.

She makes an attempt to pass him.

But one thing eats at her—how he has managed to look so healthy. It's obvious that something is up with him, but he is noticeably tanned and clean shaven, and he might have lost whatever it is that was bothering him all that time ago.

And why is it that someone spreadeagled on the ground can take it upon themselves to seem so pleased with themselves?

—Is that you? she says.

—Yes.

—It's me.

—I see that.

As subtly as she can, June unzips her bag to check the time on her phone. She composes herself to say, —Is anything matter with you?

—I mean, I'm fine, but I've had a lot going on. At least you didn't stand on me.

Something like triumph in those words.

And she is taken back to the lawn in east Cork where they made their vows, where the wind carried their promises into the afternoon, where the malaise began to set in as soon as the homemade sauce made from the homegrown mint that came with the homegrown lamb went down the front of her dress.

She tried, she did try.

—Would you like me help you up? June says.

—I'm not sure you can, he says.

—You're very conspicuous.

—It does that to you, he says.

She isn't in the mood to ask questions, but it's a slipped disk, he says. The reason husband no. 3 is lying on this single mattress is not that he is a drunk or a junkie (if he is, everyone knows it but June) but that he has a very bad back.

And who else is bothering to help him up?

Nobody.

In that regard, the mattress was a lucky find.

June gets him up and seen to (he smells like he always did: suspiciously nicely, like a prosperous altar boy) and this restores some dignity to the situation.

June needs to be on her way, and they are going to leave it like that, but husband no. 3 can't walk, he can't even sit, and she has to find a cab that he can lie down in and then he asks her to come with him to the hospital.

It's important for her to misremember how they got together (she used to clean for him) but one thing she knows is that the moment they were married, husband no. 3 was all very puzzled with June Wylie. It was as if he'd ordered a pizza with chocolate buttons on it, and when he got a chocolate-button pizza, he didn't want to eat it but didn't want to send it back either; perhaps this was why he felt the need to compliment her all the time, to prove that he'd had his glasses on when he'd read the menu.

That should have been the sign.

Another sign was him sleeping with a 'fascinating' woman who, according to the directory in his phone, went by the name of Wendy Tits.

So proud was she of her own breasts, June took to studying them in the mirror, full of admiration for anyone who'd come to be called by that name.

There was a certain judiciousness to husband no. 3 coming in behind June when she was studying herself, and roaming his hands around her, like he was trying to tell one pair from another, and using the most plausible voice to tell her of certain urges (his words, no one else's), which amounted to certain urges to sleep with other women, urges for Wendy Tits, June said, and it pleased her no end when husband no. 3 went and moved in with Wendy and her tits, which was the logic of a man who, every few months, had to get fitted for a new suit, and had to rejoin the gym he had previously abandoned, and who, every twelve months, had to get himself another Ford Granada much like his old one, and the urges were to blame. Certain urges.

He made it sound so sensible. It could have been his tone of voice (deluxe, again), but he made the outlandish—sleeping with people who weren't his wife—seem feasible.

Husband no. 3 bought his mistress an apartment in the seafront in Blackrock, and he sought June's permission.

He had a child with her and sought June's approval.

The only thing that bothered June about moving out of the house she used to do the cleaning in was having to admit she'd made a mistake in moving in there in the first place.

A few minutes later they're in Blackrock Clinic in expectation of an MRI that June would have to wait months for, and husband no. 3's phone goes.

He says hello and pauses, as if by making the running in answering the call, the rest is now up to the other person.

The silence is easily understood; Wendy Tits is on her way. June can go now.

—It would be good to see her, she says. The pair of you.

—Sure, he says.

—I've been meaning to call you, she says.

—Why's that? he says.

—There's something I'd like to say to you.

—What?

—I forget now, June says.

—It'll come back to you, he says.

—I have it now, she says. Ready?

—Ready.

—How about you both go and fuck yourselves?

—This is Ray Draper. It's been looking like we're on the go-slow after the picnic, and I hope it's not an imposition to call. I've been dropping into the Sari Grocery more than I need to, and when I go into my little box freezer, there's enough lentils to see me right. But your friend Preet said you've been jazzing up the garden a bit, so I took a little walk past, and I have to say it, June, congratulations on all the chives, but all those basins and buckets are very bad on the eye. I'm calling to offer my help, and only if you'd like it. I know wood, I was a tree surgeon. Remember my wooden house. I can build you something proper.

Oh, Ray, she thinks. You'd offer yourself as a scarecrow, wouldn't you?

She's been collecting a few terracotta pots, and the Sari has big fish boxes, and she has rinsed some of them out and in between all the pots and basins and buckets, yes, there are enough plants in enough sunlight for the bees to have a good mooch about in.

June never plans much, and it shows, rather she encourages the grasses and flowers and everything that grows there to carry on with the sense that there is space for them to get on with it on their own terms.

The thought harnesses enough energy for June to make a call of her own.

Ray answers by repeating his own number.

People of their age still have phone-voices.

When June puts it to him that she'd like to accept his kind offer, he's all business. There might even be a pencil behind his ear.

—Flowers or veg? Ray says.

—Why do you ask?

—Answer the question, please.

—I don't know, she says.

—I need to know what kind of wood to order.

—Flowers. Veg, as well.

—Untreated lumber, so.

—Do you have the tools? June says. I've a spade here, I keep it in the hall just in case.

—I have tools, thank you. Do you have soil? Or do you need me to supply that?

—I can get soil, I suppose.

—Do you have soil or not? he says.

—No, Ray, I've no soil. Why would I have soil?

—Leave it to me. I'll call if I need anything else. I'll pop round for a recce in the afternoon. We don't need to talk. All I'm in doing is sizing it up.

—I'll be here, she says.

—You don't have to be, he says.

—I live here, Ray.

—But you might be out.

It's a tight space so he's thinking two beds side by side, six foot by three foot, the size of a pool table, and no more than a couple of feet deep; she's not planting oak trees.

He'll have to level the ground, that could take a while.

He's thinking cedar, or he's thinking fir, and he's also thinking pine, for the cost. No, cedar, he prefers the smell of linseed oil to tung oil, but he'll get both.

He'll need his tools, wherever the fuck they are, he sold them for less than the price of that picnic, and he'll need a circular saw, he'll need a proper bench to put it on, and he'll need a handsaw, and he'll probably need a blade for the handsaw, and a new handle.

And he'll need something to hammer in the 4x4s, and he'll need metal corner brackets, and deck screws, and he'll probably need to ask June for her spade.

He doesn't suppose she'll invite him in, and he'll need a kettle, and a long lead to go through her living room window.

He might need a little stool, too, and a radio, batteries for the radio, and a brush for sweeping mess off the pavement, you don't want the neighbours complaining.

Anything else?

Will he be fed? He can't count on it. He'll bring a lunch, with something for her. She likes a ham roll; he'll do some of those.

The wood isn't arriving till the afternoon, but Ray's up a bit early, and he heads down with the first wheelbarrow-load.

It'll take a few runs, and he'll be in and out before anyone's up.

The thought of some proper work is bringing Ray back to himself. He hasn't slept through the night in a while, and it used to be a hard shift would send him off. And it'll be nice for June to walk out of her door to see a ridge of spuds for the digging.

He goes down to hers and then up home again.

Up and back.

Another night is opening into morning, and he gets tangled up in wondering.

He got a bit hyper at the picnic, didn't he?

This is why, hardly a week later, it feels like all of this happened last year or ten years ago, and he is standing at her gate with a wheelbarrow, and the dawn has risen without him noticing it, and he is replaying every single moment, turning each one over in the hope that it may contain a trace of a trace of something—she did take his hand, she did—that Ray can carry and keep as he drifts off later this afternoon; perhaps once he's sawn all the wood and marked up the beds.

It's not a swanky house by anyone's imagination, even his, but June's little terrace faces in the general direction of the sea and the sun is about to haul itself up over the houses on the seafront and makes its way through the village towards them.

Only here, facing southeast, will the morning light seem so pale and pink.

It's not a watercolour that's going to impress anyone, but when it's diluted in this way, it must be a nice picture to live in. June's home.

The path to the hives will have to stay clear, but he might rearrange the slabs so there's more of a road to it, with a little bench for sitting on and thinking, and talking to the bees.

There'll be enough wood for a bench, and it might be a nice surprise to show her he can do more than saw timber.

The front door opens, and there for all the world to see is June standing at her door in pyjamas and a Clash t-shirt so old and worn that it must have to belonged to someone else, her husband or her brother, someone.

Or maybe it's just hers and she's had it a while.

—I thought you'd be out at work, he says.

—It's five in the morning, she says.

Ray cups a hand around his ear. There's a deep, mournful sound coming from one of the houses, like June is living next door to a hibernating bear.

—I'd better not run the saw, Ray says. I wouldn't want to wake that one up.

June is picking at some of the herbs. It looks like she does and doesn't want to be awake. The containers are a bit higgledy-piggledy, five or six pots of chives, with their tasteful green, crowding out the rosemary.

The rosemary is near enough rotten in those pots.

The raised beds will be a new beginning.

Ray's talking about the timber that's coming. He's splashed out on some cedar, and he talks about making her something to sit on, too.

June laughs, and thinks, that'll do son. —Think of what life'd be like if I did everything you say, she says.

She rubs something in her fingers and hands it to him, and Ray's worry about revealing how he feels for June only makes him feel more of it.

It is as certain as the pink light, and the smell he doesn't know the name of.

Herb.

The snoring is still coming from next door.

—There must be plants that are good for that kind of thing, Ray says.

—Mint, she says.

—You've a powerful load of it growing already, Ray says. I remember yer man in the *Astérix* comics, boiling up bits of bark in an old cauldron.

—Nettle tea is good, it's an antihistamine. I've always got nettles.

—Grew up on them, Ray says.

And now June is awake. She was thinking of Ray in the night (magic pebbles) and she thinks: it's good to be up, and it's good to have him here. And she does keep the stone he gave her on her bedside table.

—You can come in if you like? she says.

—I'm fine here. I have my bits.

His barrow is like an invitation to an exhibition on psychopathy.

—Is that a kettle?

—Well prepared, Ray says.

—You can plug it in if you want, if you don't want to use mine.

He's had a good look through the living window already, feeling like that is as far as he will ever get, but on his walks, Ray has been picturing himself loafing around inside June's house. All the chairs he won't be allowed to sit in, and the places where you can't put your cup, and the hall, with his slippers beside hers, and the bedside table with a little radio and tissues and a book on beekeeping, and room in there for him.

—Would it impress you if I lifted a few slabs? he says.

—You don't have to do anything to impress me, June says.

—And what if I dig a nice hole?

—I'd be very happy to see that happen.

—I won't disturb the bees.

—Don't, she says.

*

There's a big, salty sky above them now and the morning is up and running. All around them, people are heading off for the day, dragging bins out and taking bins in.

They are walking out of their houses on phone calls that continue all the way down the street—people still lead busy lives—some topics are so important that they have to be discussed before you even get to the office.

Sometimes a productive day for June entails coming out here to count the snails.

Ray uses his little axe—good planning, care taking—to carve the slabs out of the ground. He is working slowly, like an archaeologist, he thinks, and he makes patient, good progress before showing June the insects that have stuck to the concrete.

The timber arrives and, sensing quite quickly that wood can very easily dominate a conversation, June leaves Ray to it.

He sets the planks on the ground; it doesn't take a second to line them up in a block on the worktable. The circular saw feels good in his hand, he's hardly guiding it at all. The timber smells like it should, and he's getting the most from the job, taking it slowly.

The happiest and saddest times involve wood: bedsteads, coffins, the bench that he is going to make for her.

Wood speaks, it can breathe, shrink and grow.

And there's one more block of timber that he wedges into the bracket, pushing it down a bit before—birdbrain, maniac—putting his hand across the blade to check it.

The plank falls in two like an apple on a kitchen counter.

When June sees an arc of blood through the door, she thinks Ray is going to die.

And Ray thinks he is going to die.

If he is going to die, it won't even be as if he knows what has happened.

He was sawing wood, he was doing the last boards, and it certainly isn't as if there is much pain, he hasn't looked yet and if you can't see it, you can't see it coming, and the pain is coming, he just hasn't felt anything yet, but when he does, he doesn't expect to feel his bones be so cold, its metal bone pain, and he doesn't expect to be entering a void, which is fine as long as you are in it, you can concentrate on the air you are staring at, but from nowhere inside himself that Ray can recognise comes a cry as dreadful as an animal's, and he will never forget the look on June's face, and the fact that he caused it.

Ray was a lollipop man there for a year, and he works in the gardens on and off, so they see to him quickly at the hospital. He doesn't have much experience of either airports or hotels, but he doesn't mind hospitals. It seems like the same thing as a hotel—you might be on your own, but you don't have to be alone if you don't want to be.

Depending on the form you're in, the interactions can go through the roof. But he knows not to catch the wrong person's eye. Whatever it is they have—the fear, it's real, hopelessness, that too, anything terminal like that—you might catch it off them.

Cheerfulness is a must, in any case.

He does very good brave face.

Did the blade catch his finger for a tenth of a second or less?

Was it a new saw or an old saw?

He gets a tetanus shot anyway, and they spray his finger and wrap it up and his entire hand gets wrapped up so tight that he can barely move his arm and the bone-pain, which was so violent and vicious, is being drowned under a wave of medicine that would give you notions of holiness.

And Ray is as small as June has ever seen him, drawing one deep breath after another. His eyes are red, and he seems to be about to say something, as usual, but they settle into a silence that says, Look at us, how did we manage to get here?

Ray has been trying to talk to her about his spiritual life being more vivid than his real life. She is not a spiritual person, but June likes who she has become when Ray is around the place and hopes that once he has come and gone (there is so much coming and going), she doesn't hate the person she goes back to being.

Hoovering under beds, getting air into rooms, drying and putting away, so many uses for vinegar. It is a good way to be, and none of that is a dream.

And June's never noticed that Ray's hand is already missing the ends of two fingers. Not even two fingers in a row!

—Maybe I could use a refresher course in using a saw, Ray says.

—We can get you on an apprenticeship, June says.

Ray drops a teaspoon and June picks it up and cleans it for him. Whenever she is down in the dumps, it soothes her to know that she can pick up after someone else. And they did muster a nice morning for themselves.

—I'll head up there to make sure everything's tidy, he says.

—I can do that, Ray.

—I've a couple of tarps we can throw over the gear for now.

—Tarps cover a multitude, June says.

They've been staring ahead, but Ray turns in the seat to face her.

—I'm sorry for being such a pain in the arse, he says.

—That's the privilege of the afflicted, she says. To afflict the rest of us.

—But I might need to take a few days off, he says. At least the wood is all cut.

—The wood is cut, and there's no mad rush. I could help, I've dug holes before.

—How long ago?

—We'll wait until your finger grows back then. I'll plant the tip in the garden, we'll grow a finger tree.

It's a relief when things go nice and quiet for a few days. She can stop worrying about Ray for a while. The company you'll get from a Ray is a bit more involved than with a Preet or a Tessa. Every time she meets a new friend, she has to adjust to a new rhythm (even with Tessa, who believes she has hired a maid as well as a cleaner).

Every time it happens, June vows to try new things, to eat new things, in different places, and at different times of the day.

Every time it happens, she is glad of the new way of getting into the water, and another way of drying yourself afterwards (Tessa pays for another hour if June takes her for a swim after she has cleaned). And every time it happens, June finds herself better off for the disruption that comes with another person's kindness.

Ray calls every night about six to say that he hopes he's not disturbing her dinner. He hopes to be back down to finish the planters soon, but his finger's still giving him gip.

He keeps asking about the bees.

On the days that she cares to think about it, June can tell her own story through the movements from the hives.

Imagine a world without bees! Ray likes to say.

June can imagine that world. It's much of a muchness with June imagining a world without June. But she follows their calendar, and has arranged herself around the milder weather, and the numbers multiplying, the preparations for swarming, and the false swarms, black and dense and frightening.

When queens start to lay less, the little bees take themselves around and about in search of forage, the ivy, the clover, the blackberries that are abundant even somewhere like Eden Villas.

Soon, it will be midsummer's night and then it will be extraction time. Now, all June needs to do is smoke rollies and eat Jaffa cakes and wait for Ray to get on with the planters.

She hasn't even told him what she has planned; or that it's a very long time since she bought a gift for anyone.

Ray ordered their dinner in Italian the other night and he had those few words of Punjabi for Preet. June was only too happy to listen to husband no. 2 speak all his languages, without any desire to join in, and she's always been so happy not to know what's being said to her, or to forget what has been said.

And she's found just the thing for Ray: an Italian language course.

While she was at it, she signed up herself.

There's something not too involving in a joint activity, but she allows herself to skip to an end in which they are speaking freely in a foreign language: Ray is ordering for her in a restaurant (she wishes he'd stop doing that); they go to the Peggy Guggenheim (and they don't choose the tour with the English translation); June talks quite briskly to the conductor on the vaporetto (and Ray applauds); they go to see a film without any subtitles (and they both fall asleep).

The ride from Ray's house to hers has become a journey to the end of his world, and even beyond that. Everything is coloured by her, everything Ray sees, all the summer sweetness, the trampolines he can imagine June jumping on, even the dogs that run up to him, and the cars that he doesn't give two shits about, he still manages to connect them to her.

See that car, see that dog, let's take a spin down to Brittas, throw some sticks.

Think of the little villages they might find, the beaches with no one on them, the lakes June can swim in while Ray holds the towel.

But something's been bothering him.

It doesn't matter what route he takes to cycle to June's; he'll pass a grandiosity of roses.

It's June, some gardens are spilling over with them. It's like a brawl, but with flowers.

Ray doesn't know why June's rose bush has no flowers on it. It's still alive, it's still a rose bush, but it's been through a lot and it's looking a small bit embarrassed for itself. It could be that it's too dark there in the corner, or it could be too wet, but flowers are there to speak to us and this is the time for the rose to proclaim itself.

If it's June and June has no flowers on her bush, that means the plant has nothing to say.

The bush gives up the ghost easily enough.

Ray pulls it out and fucks it over to the side. Looking at it, his hair is thicker than those branches. It gets him to thinking about a spruce-up for himself. He cuts it himself with the kitchen scissors. What about a rockabilly quiff?

Little Richard, Tintin, 'My Coo Ca Choo', June might help him with the Brylcreem.

And the second she comes home from work, Ray's reminded that he's a monumental fuck-up.

June takes the bush and puts it exactly where it was. To do that she has to remove the bench he's put in its place. If she even notices it, she doesn't want anything to do with it.

The rose is dead, of course it is, but she wants it back where it was.

And Ray can go.

As far as she is concerned, he was never here.

*

The first and third husbands don't count, and the second one was called Stefano, but she prefers them to go by their numbers.

June was thirty-six, they were to be married and he wanted her to choose their honeymoon destination; and because she could barely believe she was getting married again, she picked a place where he was from, and where everyone else seemed to go.

When she thought to change her mind, he wouldn't hear of it, laughing away any other ideas.

Venice, then.

They liked playing the part of husband and wife so much that a few weeks after getting back to London, June asked husband no. 2 if he'd like her to make a fruitcake like her mum used to make for her dad.

There was satisfaction to be had in measuring the ingredients and lining them in bowls—it was so reassuring to see all the ingredients in one row.

This was the primary lesson June's mother had taught her about baking: you must begin properly.

June began on the sweetened bread that later she would choke with dried fruit and rind and marzipan and a jaunty glacé cherry or two. By the time the shiny dough had proven June was thoroughly confused—even though she was certain what had gone wrong: in error she had substituted salt for sugar—and the cramps she had been experiencing for days were worsening and she was conscious of bleeding so heavily that the blood ran all the way down her legs and with the bleeding came the possibility that something was the matter.

She put up with it for a few more hours—there was no rush, she had to scrub the floor and redo the cake anyway—and that evening, without speaking with husband no. 2, she visited the hospital, where she was inspected by a young woman with cold hands and given the medication she needed. She felt strange in the days that followed, yes, but she had been only six weeks pregnant, and, by that logic, it did not matter that much.

The restaurant husband no. 2 worked at was five minutes away in Camden, and he began coming home during the day—he wasn't needed there every minute—but as it was the same time every day, she knew he was checking up on her.

Later, husband no. 2 got sick. Before he died, he asked for a few assurances. The rambling rose he bought her when she was sad got planted in their little garden in Kentish Town, and when June made the decision to come back here, she wrapped up the roots in wet newspaper, and told the man with the van to be very careful with it; and he was.

She'd promised to keep beauty around her, and if all that amounted to now was an old-woman watering a past-it rose, then she would feel a little better about the him being dead part of husband no. 2 dying.

There is space on the bench for Ray to join her. She wants to hug him, and to say goodbye. What June needs in life cannot not be supplied by Ray Draper or anyone like him.

Husband no. 2 was a lot like that.

Like he was doing you a favour, he liked to decide

what was beautiful, and when it was the right time for it to be beautiful. Not now, wait, there, see it's ready to be admired now, not in a minute, now.

Too late, gone forever.

The divinity to be found in the flower is gone because you put on the kettle or looked at your phone.

—My compliments to your carpentry skills, June says.

—Thank you, Ray says.

—No. And you've been very good at not getting under my feet, but I suppose you need to get back to all your own business.

—I can manage, he says.

—Sometime, maybe we can get back to our walks. But I'm quite tired, now. I'm very, very tired.

Now June and Ray have company. June's neighbour Tommy has come to admire the new garden. He feels like staying for a chat, by the looks of it.

—Have we had a makeover? he says. I've been thinking of getting into the beekeeping meself. Do I need to get one of them suits? Nothing wrong with dressing the part. I was below having a swim at lunchtime and there's a fella walking in his pyjamas. At lunchtime. Flip flops, towel, snorkel, this is a planned mission. So even though I'm dried and I'm out, I follows him down, and he's all you'd ever want to see in a swimmer. PJs off and of course bollock-naked underneath them and he's a fine big brute, you'd like him June, but the belly on him, that would be too much for any woman, don't ask me to describe it, he must have to send away to get them pyjamas specially made, to the place where they make clothes for circuses, but there's these little legs on him, perfectly turned ankles like you wouldn't even see in Harper's fucking Bazaar, and he's as haughty as a supermodel, a supermodel who drinks a gallon of porter for their breakfast, and does he mind if anyone's looking, any chance of a word to anyone, and would anyone dare open their mouth to him? And he's up to the top rock like he's going to make an announcement, and we all look at each other and wish we could be a little like that, half as proud of ourselves, and doesn't he walk up there like he's Mikhail Baryshnikov, and he flings himself in backwards like he's falling into the bed at home. That he can even get out of the bed in the first place is beyond the imagination.

Tommy might be talking to provide cover for June's thoughts.

—No wonder he goes about the place in pyjamas, June says. Knackered.

—Knackered is right, Tommy says. Fair fucks.

—Lovely story, she says.

—And what about you, Ray? Tommy says.

But Ray has already slipped off, without saying good-bye, and if anyone knows why he has to go it is June.

She tries to dream herself away from this garden and it's surprising how easy that can be. How lovely it can be to imagine yourself to be part of the sky. Thoughts can float and you don't have to catch them.

Some men have the knack but not Ray. There is that lingering air of old spaniel, with the animal's gentle spirit, a patient dog about to have his dinner dished out, a spaniel who can't use a saw, and with a City and Guilds in pulling out bushes.

All these years, June would begrudge anyone their happiness, but she does want Ray to have his. He'll be free now, and the hard part of it is: that may as well be an actual spaniel steering itself away down her cul de sac.

On the face of it, this is a sad moment. Desperate, in fact.

They've come to a bad end.

Was Ray weeping a moment ago? He might have been. Carefully, so as not to disturb anyone.

June is a different person for him having been there, and now a different person for him going.

—How long have we known each other, Tommy? she says.

—All my life, he says.

—Everything that has ever happened in this house comes down to one thing. Losing things. Isn't happiness just about getting things back? Everything that upsets you, it's about something that you don't have. Remember when everyone down here was all caught up with the north? Give it back, it's ours. But now I'm not sure if anyone wants it. You ever dream about an ex-girlfriend, someone you're not with? Of course, you do. You don't dream about the thing in front of you. If only I could go back, and have that back, and have him back. It's about time I stopped doing that. Other peoples' lives that I'll never live and wouldn't want to, I want those back, too. How bad must it feel not to have lived your own life, and to want someone else's. All the children who've passed through this little crescent. You, your kids. And that bush did need pulling up, but I want it back to the way it was, I want not to have neglected it.

5

The big hedge on Tivoli Road

June is glad to see the back of June.

And one of the good things about it passing midsummer is that you can say goodbye to going to bed when it's still light. Lying there when even the neighbourhood toddlers are still up and about.

The neighbourhood sounds are all very familiar.

When the wind picks up, a certain tree a few doors down makes the tender sound of a violin; she hears the animals of the vicinity complaining; the kids in no. 9 are getting better at the piano, sometimes the whole lot of them join in a singsong and it sounds hopeful and, if June is not mistaken, like they are singing this to be heard just by her; and now that Tommy has agreed to finish up his barbecues at a decent hour, whenever the gathering moves inside June finds herself straining to follow the conversation. She feels like she has had a night out herself.

*

One day, June notices someone she recognises doing something rather strange at her gate.

It's another very tasteful morning. The birds have been getting on with it, the sky is an emulsion of different potions, and, if they aren't there for the birds and the spacy happenings in the sky, why wouldn't a child be up and about to see what's to be had from the day?

Standing to attention, like one of the guards at Buckingham Palace, is Tommy's daughter Adele.

Adele is standing so still that June is not sure it's a person.

Is she watching the front door?

Then, one by one, Adele goes to inspect the raised beds. June wants to go down to say hello, but by the time she gets downstairs, Adele has gone.

The next morning, at the same time, not even six o'clock, June looks out the windows to see Adele back in position. She waves but Adele doesn't respond.

June knows from Tommy what his daughter considers a treat, so that night she leaves some out and the next morning, dead on six, she looks outside to see Adele standing at the front door eating Opal Fruits.

June goes back to bed, and the next morning, she doesn't look outside until it's time to go to work at eight, and Adele isn't there, but the next day, at the usual time, Adele is back. This time June is ready, and she runs down to the front door, and from the way Adele greets her with a certain sense of impatience, it's a disappointment that June wasn't there waiting in the first place, and that she has no Opal Fruits.

Adele turns and walks away, and June carries on with her day, as if none of it bothers her.

She isn't arsed with kids, the fairground of emotions, the mortal wounds inflicted by the wrong kind of yoghurt. But Adele isn't really a kid, she has the hormones of a middle-aged woman. So June comes home that night, and instead of going straight inside, she walks up to Tommy's house and knocks on the door.

No one in.

She walks down the drive just as Tommy pulls up in his van, with Adele buckled into the seat beside him. It's obvious from the way Tommy speaks to June that he and Adele have been discussing her.

Tommy shoos Adele inside before inviting June to take a walk with him. The moment June looks back, Adele appears at an upstairs window just like her own.

Tommy doesn't mention it, he just keeps leading June back to her house so they can talk out of earshot.

—There's to be no drama, he says.

—Now you have me worried, she says.

He begins picking at some of the weeds that have accumulated in the planter.

It's none of their business but after the little to-do with the rose bush, Tommy let it slip over dinner that he was worried about June and that they should keep an eye on her, and Adele has taken Tommy at his word.

—Am I the kind of person that people worry about? June says.

—Not a bit of it.

—Why?

—As far as I'm concerned, Tommy says, you look after us. You're here looking out for everyone.

—What does Adele say, once she's come down here to check on me?

—I've not been asking her. But she did say one thing, she said, if I keep going down there to check on her, I hope June will be alright.

—I hope June will be alright? June says.

And Ray is reminded that he is a total fuck-up.

There was a tournament coming up for experienced seniors, and Timbo is neither, so Katrina said he couldn't play in the tournament.

It was a very quick conversation.

You let one non-member in and it's no longer a club, she said. It's a public court not a club, Ray said. And people keep moving away, and dying, or giving up and getting bored, and we've a lot to learn from new talent. You've a lot to learn about how things work, Katrina said.

But Ray got the folder with all the bookings for the days running up to the tournament and he blocked out court three all day every day for the next ten days.

Ten hours a day at ten euro an hour. A grand's worth of tennis.

Ray told Katrina that he'd work for free until it was all paid off.

Come the day of the tournament, Timbo's all in a lather because there's something he wants to say: he wants Ray to be his partner in the doubles.

Has Timbo not noticed? Ray's never played a minute of competitive tennis in his life.

But Timbo wins his first match in the singles. He is strong—his neck begins halfway along his back—and he's as nervy as a setter, a little aloof, too, in the way of all the good athletes that Ray has seen. The sensation is of watching a bird slipping off a windowsill, dropping from a high floor, floating from moment to moment.

He's using a few of the tricks Ray has seen him practise, and people gather on the side-lines to observe the light shining from the twelve-year-old serving like a maniac.

When it comes to their match, it's like Timbo has three opponents, including Ray.

Tennis is all in the gestures and they haven't the languages to make themselves clear to one another. Have you ever seen a cowboy film where no one's talking except staring into the fire and having their deep thoughts? It is like Ray and Timbo are trying to talk to each other about their horses and can't think of what to say.

Ray doesn't have much to go on as it is, but it would help if he didn't shut down in the middle of points, coming to his senses only when he can feel Timbo moving around to make a shot that Ray has no chance of reaching.

A couple passing by with coffees and pastries decide that's it's a good idea to stop and watch just as it's Ray's first turn to serve, fishing around for the balls, taking one out of his pocket, putting it back, bouncing it the right number of times, blowing it straight into the net. In the time it takes for Ray to do the same with the next three serves, the mind starts to make a run for it, and the thought emerges that there was maybe a game to be had here, in spite of it all, but he is too old and worn-out enough to do anything but apologise, Ray is not necessarily working in the realms of logic here, and the thing about mistakes like whacking the ball into the sky is that you spend the next shot trying to catch up on the last one, and once you have put one mistake behind you, you open yourself to new ones, which you compare to the old ones.

You are never completely in the moment.

Ray doesn't win a single point on any of his serves. The match ends quietly, with another one into the net.

Timbo backs away when Ray goes to shake his hand, there's movement in his throat, and he gulps in assent to Ray's request to come by him. Ray kneels down to offer some words—you did well, you did, it was me—and he's not surprised to find that Timbo's absolutely heaving with tears. He's heaving with shame.

—Is this Mrs June Wylie?

—Ms.

—Sorry?

—Ms. Not Mrs.

—Not what it says here.

—Never mind. June Wylie speaking.

—I'm calling from Dún Laoghaire Rathdown Council. I have some news for you. Are you in a position to receive the call?

—It seems like that has already been happening, June says.

—Sorry?

—Please go ahead, June says. What's the news?

—I'm calling from Dún Laoghaire Rathdown Council.

—As you said, June says.

—I am calling with the news that you are being accepted for an allotment.

June says, —From the tone of your voice, I didn't think this was a good news phone call. I thought there'd been a bereavement.

—There has. That's why you're getting an allotment. Patch number 35.

June can't even remember putting her name down for an allotment.

It's two buses to get there.

Apart from sticking a crowd of bees on it, she's never known what to do with the one garden she has, let alone a second. But gardening was part of the promise to keep beauty around and it's occurred to her once or twice over the years that if she ever did get one, she might be taken back to husband no. 2 again.

After filing around and around (a bit like touring a graveyard), June finds patch no. 35, and all she sees are brambles and, probably, rats. The place hasn't been looked after at all. The raised beds (oh great) are bulging and will need an intervention (even better), but she doesn't have the slightest inkling of where to begin.

All the nice pots have been used for a game of skittles.

The only flowers worth talking about are on the potatoes.

There's rhubarb that's in need of pulling, it's gone very

droopy, and the sky is suddenly sitting very low, too, it's there on her shoulders, and it's saying, well now?

Oh, this is going to be so much work, June says in reply. I'm not a proper gardener at all. No, you'll have to work a bit harder than that, says the sky.

Imagine yourself here next year, and it's the turn of the season, you'll plant a few nice bits to eat, you're pulling up giant kohlrabi—maybe kohlrabi, why not?—and, if it's anything like this summer, it'll be hot enough to toss in a few seeds, water them in, and in a few weeks you'll have yourself a handy meal of salad leaves you won't want to eat but you'll have grown them anyway. And going from plant to plant, row to row, giving them some chat, it's for the good of the world, and everything you do at this age is for the good of the world.

There's a plot just a few along from June's which looks like a Monet painting gone mad.

There's a pair of slippers under a hedge; probably a bed for a hedgehog.

There are ribbons tied to trees and hardly a plant without a weathervane or a set of wind chimes in it.

God, it's a tip.

Sometimes June stands at the door of a house she's just cleaned, and she hopes the owners can see their own house as she does. With everything people have going on, the wear and tear of the days, there's nothing like having another person to come and look after all that you have. It makes her proud, she can't deny it, and it makes her sad, she can't deny this either, that there are so many experiences she will never be a part of.

She'll come back another day, she thinks.

June was once someone's special someone and—this is a bit much for her now—it was exactly on a grey and heavy day like this one when she met husband no. 2.

Someone walking into The Pineapple in Kentish Town at eleven in the morning and ordering a bottle of a champagne with one glass, you'd love to see it.

June still has no idea what either of them did right, but it was one of those relationships that began the moment they met. There was the repeat of a soap on mute on the TV, and June used it to give this Venetian a tour of the British Isles.

Not everyone from Liverpool is a thief, not everyone from Scotland is a miser, and not everyone from Ireland is as friendly as they'd have you believe.

—Not everyone from Venice is a merchant, husband no. 2 said.

There and then, June decided to do something she had never done before. She wanted this person to see only the good in her. She didn't know where to begin, but the free packet of scampi fries seemed to be a nice touch. A regular wee bistro we have here, she said, and the champagne's a bit wet on its own.

He thanked her, solemnly, by saying he would treasure the moment forever (yes, he had his moves).

She always avoided asking too many questions of her customers, but now that she'd found this man, she wanted to know everything there was about him.

Husband no. 2 had come to London to work in a Venetian restaurant that was supposed to be more authentic than the ones at home. Not a bit of it, he said. Besides, the prices were four times as much as they'd be in Italy, and husband no. 2 detested the notion of food as a luxury.

Hence, the champagne before lunch.

The basics.

It was a very basic bottle of champagne, June had to agree, and by the time he was finished with the story of what people like Joan Collins and Edna O'Brien liked for dessert (champagne), there were two glasses out, and the next bottle was on June Wylie.

The thoughts move a bit of the blood in her; in a body that was once a source of so much pleasure and fun.

Husband no. 1 had been a brute, but the sex she had with husband no. 2—which began the day they met; they weren't long in breaking each other in—was full of kindness. She'd wake up every morning to breakfast on a tray delivered by a lovely person who wouldn't shut up about how much he loved buttering her toast. It was confusing, unsettling, and more lovely than June can think about now.

The fifteen years they shared was only the beginning, she'd thought, but happiness's trick is to have you believe it will go on forever. You might think these memories would give her a lift, and they do, but it's been so long since she's had love and kindness on the brain.

This is all Ray's fault.

And there's someone standing right behind her, mesmerised by the wind chimes, too, perhaps.

—I can see what you're up to, they say. Don't worry,

I've never seen anyone come up here and know where to begin.

The owner of the messy garden is called Patricia. She is wearing three or four denim shirts, one on top of the other. She has bad teeth and good posture, and she's rolling a tiny cigarette with her big gardener's hands.

The smile indicates that Patricia has seen a lot more than June looking confused at a bunch of broken pots, and it says that she is the kind of sassy madam who'd go over to the scariest guy in any room and tell him his fly is undone and his wellies are too new.

Patricia assumes June wants the tour of the garden.

The patch smells bready and of warm ground and now the sun is battling through, the overall effect is of liquid honey, the processed kind that gleams more than any other.

And the change in the light makes Patricia seem all flushed and a bit too eager.

She uses an old iron bath to collect rainwater that gets taken home to wash in, and the soap she uses in the bath is made from old cooking oil.

—I'll bring a bar up for you, Patricia says.

—That'd be nice, June says.

—Just a small donation. There's a tin hanging on the back fence. Pay what you can. It might seem a bit hand-made, but I'm a make do and mend person.

The phrase—make do and mend—is supposed to make June feel relaxed, and, true, she has come up here in the clothes she slept in.

She says, —I'm sure there's plenty of people with more energy who'd do a better job with it.

But Patricia is insistent that June make a go of the allotment. She will help, everyone mucks in. June can invite people to help her.

Preet might come, Tessa might come, Tommy might bring Adele so that they can stand around eating Opal Fruits and staring at the raised beds. This will all be so, with hand on heart, June can say that she has made a go of it.

But there is now the great weight of disappointment between them, but perhaps no more disappointing than any conversation Patricia gets herself involved in. She must meet these weak pilgrims every day.

She stops to fuss with some corn that's been dragging its feet.

—Aren't you supposed to pick these later in the season? June says.

Patricia nods curtly, while puncturing a kernel with one of her big fingernails.

The liquid should be milkier by now. It's also about the ripeness, and the balance between sugar and acid, all the ways in which a plant can happily grow and what can be done to help it along, and how everyone could do with a good winter that doesn't confuse everyone by zigzagging in and out of spring.

—The earth needs its rest, Patricia says.

She picks a plum and eats it and keeps on going.

It hasn't taken much to convince June she won't be growing plums and corn of her own.

They've made their way all around now, and June is ready to hit the road. But the sky is heavier than before and she's sure to get soaked on the way to the bus.

She imagines the rain pelting down, and Patricia with her face up to the sky, mouth open to collect more rainwater, and June imagines herself at home, listening to the radio and she imagines waiting on another round of honey and toast.

—Are you on foot? Patricia says.

She is checking that June doesn't have a car.

You get points for there being no car. Medals for going around in sandals in the winter.

—Bus, says June. Or thumb.

—I'll drop you home, Patricia says.

June doesn't know what age anyone is any more, and suddenly Patricia looks tired, and as old as the Dublin mountains. As soon as she gets behind the wheel of her Polo, the little car asserts its dominance, and Patricia becomes a hesitant child in a grownup's shirt.

—I hope we'll see you again, Patricia says.

—You never know, June says.

—I don't know what happens to me when I get up here. I think the garden can sense who I am, and it responds accordingly. I think it might do the same for you.

And June really enjoys the ride home, without so much of a second thought about what will become of this person—and their ribbons and their soap and their bath awaiting its fill of rainwater—and what'll happen when June gets home and in the door, what she'll do once she's had her tea, or what she'll say to the person from the council when she calls them to say she doesn't want anything to do with the allotment.

*

99

This little car really has the better of Patricia.

June can see them being stuck in it until the end of time, the survivors of a disaster movie, the last ones left alive, eyes fixed on the horizon, not saying very much, and not having to, because Patricia has already done all the talking that can ever be done.

—You see a lot of people living outside this time of the year, hanging hammocks, putting tents in the garden for the kids. Have you ever stopped to think what might happen if we all had to live outdoors? You'd see a lot less strife, fewer domestic incidents. Cooking on the fire, finishing your dinner and putting the leavings straight onto the compost heap. What about doing the dishes? It's raining, just put the plates out. Dishes out on the lawn.

It seems to be the case that being a gardener turns you into a philosopher; owning a trowel allows you to say weird things to strangers.

Then June screams, —Stop the car.

Ray is standing there on Tivoli Road. The breeze is carrying smoke from a barbecue so that it looks like dry ice from a Duran Duran video.

The heavens have opened, and he's been finding shelter under a massive overgrown hedge with the most buckmental purple flowers. The hedge is so big that there is a good chance that he has not seen them drive past.

June squeezes Patricia's hand to say thanks for the chats and the lift, so long, and she steps out of the car and crosses the road.

How June has missed her Ray.

And now she is in his eyeline.

One of them takes a step then the other. One of them curtsies then the other.

How they wish the other could see what they see and how they see it.

His face is near hers, hers when it is near his.

How time has been slipping from her—how the years run, how sharply they fall—and she has been given one more chance to resume a life she has lost track of.

Ray's face when he misunderstands a cue, the change in it when she is close to him, thinking of kissing him, and the surprise in them both as she places her hands around his waist.

He's very glad of the closeness to her.

June's face is alive, the demands it is making.

The frosting of the hair on her chin, the little looseness below her ear, as though someone was in a hurry folding pastry.

All the love that they have been holding for one another, it has been here all this time, and they will carry it onwards in these shapes.

The part of her that Ray has always wanted to kiss he is kissing now, not just the hard-to-find places but the obviousness of cheekbones, the diagrams they make, the muscular form of her top lip as it finds his, and they are kissing, that's what this story has been moving towards.

The absurdity of her skin up close, paleness in all this brightness, and nothing but time and fear in a moment that may be too much for Ray as he holds the back of June's head, so shapely, and it is the skull that holds the brain that makes the decision at the same time as he does; the timing, they could work on that, it has taken them a while and it takes him a moment to resume it, the summer's warmth in her skin and all the things she does that says who June Wylie is and, true, she has been in funny form lately, but it might pass, and all the attentiveness that Ray has ever shown her, she will return it, she will double it, and it will multiply, June will make sure he feels the difference, and it isn't unreasonable to say that telepathy is occurring, and it is as certain to him as it is to her and to feel it going is to know that it will return and to know that the world doesn't do this all the time, it can't provide these moments for just anyone.

And why does a kiss in the rain always signal the end of a story?

6

Beginners' Italian

They're agreed on activities. The library, exhibitions, but nowhere north of Booterstown.

They're agreed on a good walk every day, from the cove to the beginning of the pier, or the up and down one of the piers. They're agreed on only meeting once June has had a sleep after work, and that's fine by Ray.

They're agreed on not being in and out of each other's houses.

They're agreed on no newspapers, which are full of news and therefore to be avoided. What's in the news that you don't need to stay on the wrong side of? The tomato growing on the International Space Station. The king of Tonga dying peacefully. You can't read about the sad sheep of Cromarty Firth without seeing all the other stuff, the dispossession, the poisoning. And all the burning catches in the throat.

What's all this about life getting better?

They're agreed that Ray will stop telling June she looks lovely.

They're agreed on hugs and handshakes but no more kissing for now; the small matter of losing the run of themselves on Tivoli Road in the rain is not to be discussed, there being plenty of time for all that in the next life.

They're agreed on there being regrets, but don't ask them what.

They're agreed on yellow roses, lovely.

They're agreed on scones, ditto.

They're so at one with the attractiveness of the notion of dying in your sleep that they—briefly—discuss the pros and cons of murder suicide. Not something to joke about. No.

They're agreed on Christmas being for the children, they're agreed on children singing.

They're agreed on the thought of taking a trip, but where might take a bit of discussion. June was in Venice for her honeymoon, they're agreed this was all a very long time ago.

They're agreed that it's not that frightening to think of some things being your last.

They're agreed that this world isn't what they thought it would be, but that they'll take what they can get and, when the time comes to be not alive that the spirit will take off for all the places that have been barred to it, and they're agreed on how sensible that sounds.

They're agreed on this being quite enough to go on.

One day, as they're kicking the wall at the end of the east pier, and they've just seen the mailboat on its way to Holyhead, and they've discussed taking a day trip to Wales, and they've decided against taking a day trip to Wales, June has a surprise for Ray.

She doesn't want to talk about her garden—such a mess that was, with the poor rose and Ray's poor finger.

Even at the time, June did wonder what the hell she was doing getting them language lessons, and she is worried that it will be too much like school, which she hates, and that she won't manage it and Ray will.

He says he likes the idea of learning Italian.

—I'm just glad we get to do new things together, he says.

—There is that, she says.

—We know how not to have a picnic, how not to order a burger and chips, how not use a saw.

—You'll get the hang of it, she says.

—I could do with speaking better English, so I'd understand people better. But if I learn Italian, I need to imagine myself there. Going about my daily business. Having a coffee, having another one, getting palpitations, flopping around on their nice marble floors.

—I've been there, she says. I told you.

—You told me.

—With my husband, she says.

—Venice is an awful romantic place to go on your own.

She says, —Until you came along, I'd done a very good job of shutting all that down. It was like avoiding sugar, or drinking spirits, or looking in the mirror.

—You know best, Ray says. There are flights. We could get on one.

—Don't think so, she says.

—Next best thing, he says. Let's learn Italian and never go there.

They go the new library in the seafront and get all signed up to use the computers. There's a row of folk just like them, looking up their lineage, being proud of or aghast at their lineage; nimbly checking the time of the Aircoach; finding out how to remove leaves from the gutter, finding someone who will do that for them; writing poems as Gaeilge, translating poems, sending them to lunchtime radio shows on which they'll hear them being read out live and then listen back to using the big headphones you get in the library.

Ray gets settled in at the computer. He wants to see the world. He goes along the wiggly street in San Francisco then up Via Condotti in Rome—nice shops—then, wondering where Miranda might be, he tries a few neighbourhoods in Melbourne. Very nice, very like here, more nice shops.

That takes two minutes.

A few days later, they find themselves down the road in beginners Italian at the Further Education Institute.

Ray and June are sitting side by side at a school table. She's treated them to new pens, and Aisling copybooks. Everyone there has just been on their holidays to Italy, and it's oddly as though Francesca, the instructor, is still on hers.

Francesca makes it seem all very leisurely. She's at pains

to explain that there'll be no grammar, but by the end of the month, everyone will be making phone calls to estate agents in the Marche, where Francesca has just been, and writing emails to Italian radio shows.

Very soon they'll be unleashed for madcap antics they'd never thought imaginable.

But Ray is wearing a very fixed expression that June has never seen before. It's like she's trying to get the attention of the swot who finds everything interesting and worth his while, even the grammar, and who'll help her with the homework (which she'll get them caught cheating at).

Only when she whispers that they'd be as well learning Irish does Ray crack a smile.

It won't be like school, he's thinking.

They're adults talking to adults, and he'll get a good few interactions, and he'll get the bit of Italian, and he'll do what you're supposed to do—no grammar—and he'll do it as best as he can.

Only the loopers at Ray's school did art, and since he was a total space-cadet he got to do art. In the kitchen at home there was a map of the universe and all his life, Ray had his breakfast under it, eating his porridge and wondering about the world and all the things he could do in it. He daydreamed; he drew maps, he had good hands, loose wrists, he drew diagrams, spectacular graphs, instructions for physics experiments that could have been magic tricks, drawings more accomplished than anything he could do now.

June is looking over at him, her arm's moving around the back of his chair. Ray hopes she's enjoying the class.

Francesca is making it fun; she is making it easy.

I am here on holidays, you are here on holidays, they are here on holidays, the cat is not here on holidays, the cat is eating our pasta, the cat is not supposed to eat our pasta.

It all sounds like grammar.

Francesca walks up and down the rows, the cheerful young abbess. She misses them the first time but her double take at Ray's missing fingertips is disguised as interest in his handwriting. His Ws are like Ns.

There's the urge to stuff his hands in the pockets of his shorts.

If Ray was still a little boy, this would all be very embarrassing. He stands quietly, and very quickly he walks across the room. He did have good hands, a quick pencil, but long before any happenstance with saws, they were raw from the scraping he'd give them.

Tá rud éigin caillte agat, tá rud éigin caillte agat, tá rud éigin caillte aige.

He's not cut out for school, is he?

June finds Ray outside, and she wonders, how will they make themselves understood if they ever go to Italy? They'll just have to gesticulate and point, she says. That's the cat who's eating my pasta.

But Ray is not being himself.

—Is there anything you would you like to do? she says.

Ray doesn't know. These desperate galloping feelings have lasted too long, and they're still doing their work in him. And maybe there is something Ray would like to do.

If they want to go for a daytrip, there's a bus that goes to Glendalough, there and back in an afternoon, and from there they can take any number of walks.

He would like her to see what he used to do, and where he did it, forgetting for a minute that he can hardly walk and that he hasn't been near a tree in twenty years.

The great outdoors, it's a subject for them to ponder.

On the bus they decide on their favourite bird: swallow (perky, likes to travel); favourite bird: owl (shy).

Favourite animal: otter (they seem to enjoy themselves); favourite animal: bear (never met one, would like to).

Favourite tree: oak (the age they get to); favourite tree: oak (durable wood).

Favourite plant: chive (for the bees); favourite plant: rambling rose (don't ask).

Favourite kind of water: sea (it's the sea); favourite kind of water: river (sweeter water)

Favourite thing to do at the beach: get in (why not?); favourite thing to do at the beach: hold the towels (some-one has to).

They don't do least favourite things.

They walk from the visitors' centre to the lower lake, and to the edge of the lake, and Ray asks if they can keep walking to the falls. He points out the circling hawk (looking for snakes; yes, he says, they exist) and the wan-dering goat who patrols the paths to the falls.

Ray and the goats were very well acquainted.

June wants to know how he ever got into the forestry, and why (the quick answer: Ray ended up in the Harbour Bar in Bray with some fella who put him onto some labouring work, and six weeks later asked him if he'd ever used a chainsaw), not realising that Ray stopped being a tree surgeon for better reasons than he had for being one, since, in so many ways, the job involves not a love for trees but a disregard for them.

He was too long working that out.

Half a lifetime of not saying that you're scared of heights; the gusts when you're hanging by your bollox fifty feet up in the air; the handsome looking tree that's dead on the inside; thirty years of having your breakfast in a garage forecourt; the amount of time you end up trimming hedges; the missing bits of his fingers; people asking you for firewood; chainsaws.

—It's a wonder I've never gone deaf, he says.

—Sorry? she says.

There has been some rain in the night, somewhere, and the falls themselves are more vigorous than he was expecting, and June and Ray have the place to themselves.

They climb the fence so they can sit on the bank facing the water. The landscape is doing its bit, the sun glowing obligingly through the leaves. There's a nice bit of dazzle.

But Ray is not himself, no.

He wants to lie down on the moss, sleep there.

The tears are real but feel put on.

—Anything you want to talk about? June says.

—Another time, Ray says.

The hazards of looking back over your shoulder; it makes the moment you're in a whisper less substantial. It is a beautiful and easy thing to keep all the parts of your life apart, he is sure of that, and surprised by it and, in fifty years, he has never told anyone this story.

After Miranda, the Australian, or it could have been before Miranda, came the abbey.

You go through discernment, but you're not yet a novice.

Postulants are told to be patient. You will hear from God, you will hear when the time is right.

Three months in the abbey made him feel invincible and very, very patient, six months in the abbey he was so tranquil he was barely alive, a year in the abbey and the brain almost shut down, it almost ceased functioning.

He was listening, truly listening, but it was becoming clear that while Raymond Draper was a patient young man, he was not an alert young man. All things considered, this was not a sussed young man.

There isn't much Ray remembers now, but the one peculiar thing he will allow himself to think about is the way the postulants were invited to join the monks at vespers.

He would stand there, miming so dutifully and meticulously, until one of the monks, Brother Placid he was called, invited him to take the lead on 'Salve Regina', and the first thing was, the monks wore robes and Ray was in an anorak, and it wasn't even brown, like a set of robes, it was a blue anorak.

And Ray couldn't sing—you can love music and not be able to sing—and he barely made it through the first line before he walked past everyone and out of the church, forgetting to genuflect or even bow (why does he remember that?), and he hung around in the refectory waiting for someone to come, and nobody came, and he went to his room and had the can of orange he'd been saving, and then he walked back to the chapel but by that time everyone had gone, and he thought he'd make himself useful by tidying up the missals before evening prayer, and he made sure every pew was well-supplied before he could go and find Brother Placid to apologise, but Ray went looking for him, around the sacristy, and outside, but no one was there, not one person, so they might have been hiding on him, it might have been a prank, and it wasn't until he reached the sports pitches that he started to feel that feeling, the one he didn't name until much later, the running one, the galloping motion in his chest, and he assumed it was just going to take him over, but the blood wouldn't stop running, it just kept moving around, ending up in new parts of his body and his head, and of course the blood being in those new places meant Ray was done for, everywhere, but in the abbey most of all, and before he had even started, the end can come at the start, but with all the strangeness and silence and cold, he hadn't heard from God, and so it wasn't easy to hear anything much, even telling yourself that you couldn't hear, he couldn't hear that, and if he wasn't able to hear anything else, how could Ray hear himself say it was time to go to bed without talking to anyone.

No evening prayers.

No saying thanks for the invitation to sing.

The next thing he saw as he left the grounds was the senior rugby team running drills under the floodlights, giving out shite to one another. When they were finished, the players lay on their backs, rotating their legs in the air and laughing their heads off, and perhaps, if Ray was to say any more about the abbey now, perhaps he should try to make it all seem more humorous.

June appears to have fallen asleep, lulled into it by the waterfall.

She's dozing, her chin has dropped to her chest.

They might have a walk to St Kevin's Bed when June wakes up, but this place is not what it was, it's not saying a thing to him, and he doesn't have many more details about the abbey, how long he hung on after that night, a week, or two, if Ray Draper went to any more vespers, when he left, how he left.

After a few minutes, June raises her head, coming to, and, like a bird on a branch, looks around herself in all directions. Forgetting that she is being observed, she starts to blow her nose, nostril by nostril directly onto the ground.

—Lovely, June says. Sorry. Was I out for long?

—Just long enough, he says.

—But I didn't mean to drop off on you. I've had a nice time today.

—Me too, he says.

—If you keep on dragging me to these awful places.

The lake and the lakeside are completely deserted when they get back. The water is shining, and light is gilded enough to think to take a photograph; the notes of summer's end showing up nicely on June's skin and in the thought that this is a moment worth marking.

Ray loves to take snaps on his phone, and she wants him to take her photo standing in the water. They are paddling in water so shallow that it takes an age to wade up to her knees.

She stands there, arms spookily straight by her sides.

He takes one, two, three, four, five, ten versions of the same pose. If their friendship is real, Ray's life now depends on where she is and where she might be, and it is now that bit truer for them having been here.

After a variety of poses (sitting on a rock, forefinger to the side of her mouth, her feet trailing the water), Ray can imagine what she might have looked like when she was younger, thirty, forty, fifty years ago, and when Ray Draper takes a walk through his life, he sees more of these Junes; in his little flat, and in his teens and twenties and thirties and on, and there is all this life bursting out of her, even when she's reading her book, say, or when she's chopping wood, sunbathing, cycling a bike just like his, and in all of this she's more alive than he's ever been.

Ray wades into the water so June can see the pictures he's taken. Love is the subject of the photographs; June is certain of that. Who is to know how life has treated someone?

—Let's spend the night together, she says.

Very quickly Ray says, —We said we weren't going to.

—I'd like to know what it's like to wake up beside you.

—Like waking up next to a boulder, Ray says.

Then he takes some water in his cupped hand, and June

holds hers out to be filled. He fills her hands with water, and she lets him drink from it. When he is finished, June keeps her hand there, clamping it over his mouth.

Her hands are wet and cool, his face is wet and warm.

All they know now is that it would hurt her to hurt him, and it would hurt him to hurt her.

June puts her lips to his, and all Ray can do is think of the mouth he is kissing, and they are struck all the while by the way in which the course of a life can change, as though lives have personalities and, by meeting this person, theirs have changed entirely.

7

What kind of tomorrow would you like?

The planters are thronged. The courgettes go blousy almost overnight, but the stripes and patterns are cosmic enough to keep you gawping for the whole day. She might take up painting, just to do a picture of her vegetables.

There's one that's the size of a giant clog, she'll stuff it with Bolognese for their lunch.

Bolognese in a big marrow, Ray. If you know you know.

She goes inside to see to things, and there's a very nice kind of light in the kitchen, that she doesn't recognise.

It's a carousing light.

Ray's coming for lunch, with the possibility of dinner, and with the possibility of etc.

She's been going back and forth over different ideas for afters. It isn't anything she would eat, but June prefers to make cakes as if they are for children: enough chocolate or cream to float a barge on, overdone with fruit—both don't tend to work, but sometimes they do.

She could ask Ray.

He's only been on the phone every hour on the hour.

I'm a bit nervous, he's been saying.

In what way? she's been saying.

They're agreed that they've done very well to get this far. And they're agreed that they are more in their own lives now that the other is in it. And they're agreed that the kiss will be it.

There is another room across the hall, and if they do decide that perhaps he'd prefer to sleep in there, that's where Ray will be. June's put it to him as a kindness, and Ray seems to have accepted that she is trying to save them from any embarrassment.

Wouldn't you like the company at night? he said.

I don't know, she said.

It feels like you are company for me already. You in your bed in your house, me in mine.

I could be your companion, he said. You'd be awake before me or I might be awake before you, and we could be there with a smile. It might be nice to wake up to a smile.

Would you do that, she said, sleep in someone's bed just to smile at them in the morning?

She doesn't even think Ray will be a cake person, but June whips more cream and squishes more fruit into the jam to make it seem like her own. Then she leaves the cake alone so she can focus on upstairs.

She airs the bedroom a bit more.

There's a bee on the sill. Good to see that they are still getting out and about. There are always a few dossers but enough of the hard workers are out on patrol.

No one else has slept here since she moved back in after husband no. 3, who spent one night under this roof and never again. She hasn't been sitting there waiting for it, but every now and again June has felt the pull of love and always she has been mistaken. What is it and what does it look like?

Husband no. 2. coming home with the news that it was going to be all over.

Husband no. 2 sending her off to the garden centre.

No, love is bees, love is one bee, love is one bee bumping around on your windowsill, minding its own business.

Perhaps they have sussed out that she's as nervous as Ray will be. Perhaps they'll remember him as the man who tore out the rose bush.

She goes down for a chat with them, and a few of the bees come out to bump around. It's a lovely thing when one of them seems interested in you and, nice bees that they are, they do listen to her, but today the bees are more concerned with themselves.

Then Ray floats in quietly enough to catch her by surprise. He's on foot. She was expecting to hear the wheels of the bike.

It takes her a moment to absorb that fact of him being there with a cake. Ray undoes the ribbon on the box and presents a Victoria sponge ten times nicer than the one waiting for him in the kitchen.

—This can only mean one thing, he says.

—What's that?

—Cake for breakfast.

They go inside, and the nice light has gone, and now Ray is in her kitchen, and he has his eyes on everything.

The stainless-steel ashtray came from The Pineapple, which is still going, she thinks, and the ashtray is all she has to show, pretty much, for half a life spent in London. That's all gone, but the rollies, she can't even get into why she's still at them.

She brushes her teeth a lot, but unbeknownst to itself, a mouth can give off bad mists, sometimes a mouth could do with a good dust.

Never kiss anyone is one rule, not if you want to keep at the smoking.

June offers Ray the tour, she wants him to see the set-up upstairs.

The bannisters are made from three different types of wood (thanks to husband no. 1) and, on his way upstairs, Ray is quick to offer a solution. It won't cost much, and it won't take long.

—Unless you like it the way it is, he says.

—I'm just used to it, she says.

—It's up to you, he says.

—It's an idea, she says.

And at the top of the stairs, June shuts the door across the hall. She takes Ray's hand and leads him into her room.

She's been so afraid to have him here, but the open window is like a screen you're drawn to stare at, and she likes the way Ray makes space for her in the room, hanging outside to look down on the planters, talking about the timber he'd use for the banister.

—Just in case you're about to ask, she says. Nothing ever happens in here.

The thought is an invitation to lie down in their clothes on the bed, and two seconds later they are in the kitchen slicing cake.

June gives Ray the same napkin six times.

Ray is eating for hours. It's like watching a dog clear its bowl, scraping the empty plate so long then looking up at her for more.

It isn't just that he wants to try both cakes, it's that they don't know how to eat and not talk. He'd talk all day with his mouth full, and it's the eating, talking, talking, eating; separate transactions that require different types of energy that are impossible for June to combine.

It's eleven in the morning and the exhaustion is a reminder of how long June was doing this for, sat there begging the universe for someone to walk in and eat and talk at her table. It is such a long time since she considered life to be fair, and as soon as other people are involved, their hearts, her heart, you must think of what's fair. If she lets anyone in here, when the time comes, they'll die on her, and they'll die on her, here, or she'll die on them, and when the time comes, it won't be fair.

June has her sensible moments, and her mad moments, and she feels a mad one coming on.

It will move onto something less mad, it will become

more manageable, she knows that, and Ray will carry on being so nice about the napkins, and all the happier for a seat at someone's table, but the unfairness of husband no. 2 dying attacks her with so much viciousness that she has to go to the back door to converse with the bins, as if they haven't heard everything already.

—I have an idea, she says.

—How about no more cake for at least five minutes? Ray says.

He thinks he knows what's going on, but he hadn't thought she'd be so fidgety.

And her idea is that children like cake.

They'll go and see if Adele wants to help them out. Tommy won't say no, either.

Adele is the little peeper June's told him about, but she is very good, and she gets little sprigs of mint for their plates. June looks to be coming out of herself, too.

She'd gone into herself but now she's out again, Ray thinks.

It's not a picture anyone has ever sought to draw around Ray Draper, but he might burst at the thought of June with a young one of her own, bent over a pram, singing little ditties, the little bag of carrot-sticks in her backpack, the jab of a hankie at a snotty nose.

June with all her little ones around her.

It's been a good idea to take the cakes for a walk. Ray has been invited into a room where nothing is expected of him other than to sit and watch and listen. June talks to Adele about her new school uniform, the reasons why jumpers are supposed to be itchy (so you don't fall asleep in your lessons), and why lunch boxes are rectangular.

Loaves of bread are rectangular, there'll be hell to pay if Tommy dares come home with round bread ever again.

Adele gifts a list of the things she wants for her packed lunch. Imagine talking to your father like that! Imagine talking to your father at all. Ray's parents were just from the enigmatic side of the equation. You were brought up to mind your own business—eat your porridge, don't burn your mouth—and not to be seen enjoying yourself. You'd have to explain that to a child nowadays.

But this is all magical.

Ray's imagined dying before—dropping the needle on the Etta version of 'I'd Rather Go Blind'. Or after an hour on the courts in some April sun. Or freewheeling down Glenageary Road with his hands off the handlebars. Or eating fettuccine Bolognese in Minnelli's. Keeling into the fish counter while buying mackerel pâté for a picnic.

But he could also go now and if that happened, Ray Draper could, if he had to, say that he had done okay for himself.

A nice bit of cake (it looks like Tommy is getting out the ice-cream), some nice people, and June.

Never has a face fitted together so well.

Is he mumbling to himself? He is. But it's the face that's giving him the mystical notions. She's a picture, alright, but it's not even physical, it's a presence, a melody, a fuck load of lovely vowels strung together by a God in a good mood, one who knew what they were doing.

Ray wants to roar it out.

He has even managed to stop being in love with bits of her.

When they get back to hers (the bees are still flitting in and out), June bends to see what's ready to pick from the planter, and they begin to talk of the summer, and what they might do next year, feeling the draw of putting in some raspberry canes in place of the rose and the sense of the garden being a little more alive because of them, and even she has to admit that it's a lovely thought, and why Ray might have come up with it.

—Ray, I'd like to go up and have a sleep, she says.

—I'm very full of cake, he says.

—Meaning?

—I'd just like to sleep.

—Let's go, she says.

—It's three in the afternoon.

—I know, she says.

When they make it up to the bedroom, Ray takes his bag to get his pyjamas, but June thinks they can just get undressed and lie down on the covers for a while. All the tenderness between them immediately makes itself available, and they let themselves be naked with each other. Ray can't stand himself but it's right that June sees him at just the moment as he sees her.

It's their own bodies they notice first, the loose, dry, knuckle parts that you don't like to look at but now the other person has seen.

They are sitting side by side with their arms touching. Is the back of his neck like hers?

They're both animals who've seen a lot of work.

One of them makes a joke about the whiteness of the sheets.

There are parts of June's arms Ray has never seen, and the paleness of her breasts, all the workings behind them, and how she may be naked, but he is still taken in by her face.

The world is now very small.

Ray waits as she shuts the curtain, quickly but not quick enough so he doesn't get it all. When she reaches up, there is the assertion of the muscles in her back, and the skin in her middle stretches out, but Ray prefers her stomach when she bends to sit.

The glamorous folds.

He's covered himself with a pillow, but she doesn't want one.

June has seen her fair share of naked men, and when she pulls Ray a little closer to her, she senses how nervous he is, helpless and cold, but this is the right thing for them to do. They sit quietly on the bed, and with a 'may I', Ray places his hand on her thigh, and she smiles because it's exactly what she wanted him to do.

June moving to lie on her side is an invitation for Ray to hold her from behind, and they feel the draw of the clean sheets and the new pillows and the moment accommodating them, the breeze from the garden and the outside sounds making themselves part of the arrangement; these things becoming pronounced when he explores her with his hand.

The afternoon is happening outside. There's a harbour not too far away, and a beach with people throwing themselves into the sea.

One or two of June's bees have popped in, and not finding much of interest, entertain themselves by arcing through the air. The shapes they make, the flight paths are insane.

June can't move much of herself but now and then she twists herself to look over her shoulder, and Ray nods.

I'm here, they are saying.

Ray wants June to take the initiative from him, but her murmur indicates that he should continue.

His leg is in between hers; his thigh is sitting in between her legs.

Parts of her are warm and parts of him are cold.

June has an impulse to guide him, and for a moment it does seem as if she is gripping Ray's hand.

Hello, they both say at the same time.

They can hear each other breathing. Ray can hear June and June can hear Ray. The hurt can hear each other. And if they are now in the love part of love, this is as far as they will go.

They both have the same question.

Is this how souls seep into one another?

It's nearly dark when they wake up to the cheerful thought that lunch, only six or seven hours late, can create a little event in the evening.

There is always a specific moment, just at this time of the night, when everything shuts down on you. All the little lamentations can pile up on themselves.

It's usually quite straightforward: give up and wait for tomorrow.

While June gets the food ready in the kitchen, there

is the new music of Ray banging around in the shower. When he appears at the kitchen door, June goes over to smell him.

She is not going to pass comments on everything, but it's the trace of your own shampoo on another person. Beginning with her fingers at his forehead and running all the way to his neck, she runs her hands through his wet hair, and she is thinking about them being upstairs together.

They got that far, no difficult demands were made, and she wonders how many of their days can be arranged in these innocent shapes?

She puts the stuffed marrow down in front of them, Ray crosses his hands over his chest like he's being funny, even though that's not what's happening, and June can see what Ray can't—he is a beautiful man, and however crumpled they might be now, when you sleep the creases disappear.

—Today's been a bit back to front, he says.

They can't sleep. As soon as they leave her house for a walk, they agree that today has felt a like a lifetime. It's hardly autumn at all, summer won't end, and at two in the morning, the sparkle that settles on the seafront seems available to all. The houses lit in ways to show that everyone is asleep.

You could only guess if anything momentous has gone on down here today.

And resolve returns to you at the oddest hours.

Perhaps Ray's courage has been deepened by today, perhaps it's them being out here alone, but he could walk along the seafront every night and never have the nerve to do what he is about to do.

They pass Tessa's house, catching a glimmer of themselves in the window of the BMW parked outside, and they stop to wave at themselves in the reflection. Whenever they walk along roads like this Ray feels he has nothing for June.

He has to be able to give someone something.

The only real thing Ray has ever owned is a necklace of pearls owned by his grandmother, left to him by his mother. When his mother died—was it fifty years ago?—he used to carry it with him, he'd go around with them like a set of rosary beads.

Weathered, saltwater, pale purple and pink like the seeds from a strawberry. They were strung and knotted on fine silk thread that disintegrated on him so that for years he went around with about thirty pearls in his pocket.

They'd been in an old pair of shoes for years. It was only when Ray thought he might put on some desert boots for June that he remembered them.

He'd always known he was going to do something special with them.

Wild pearls, real ones, something about holding them up to the light; and light was it, he has a feeling that some people go through life with more of it than others.

Last week, Ray sold the pearls for a nice few quid, and he's been thinking they could go somewhere.

They can go wherever they want, they could fly out tomorrow, they could go to the airport now.

—I've got an idea for a bit of a jaunt. I don't want you flipping your lid, now.

—That's one way to get me to do exactly that, Ray.

—I've got you a little something, he says.

—Is it another pebble? June says.

—It's very far from a pebble, he says.

—Just tell me, please.

—I know what you're going to say. Stop giving me things. So this is not a gift for you. It's for me as much as it is for you, that I get to go there with you. I had a windfall, so to speak, and I'd like to take us somewhere.

Venice, he's saying.

And lovely man that he is, Ray is looking into her eyes, as deeply and meaningfully as he can, and with everything he can muster, and all June wants to do is get in Tessa's BMW and drive over him in it.

It would probably take a few goes to run him over, the bastard.

Oh, she wants to shake him so hard.

She wants to kick him straight in the balls.

But something changes in the way Ray is looking at her. There's a strange, sweeping light in the sky, a car coming slowly around the bend. It's a taxi, and the driver swings up onto the other pavement. The car is full, but he's looking for a fare for the way back.

June turns and walks. She had no idea how this could have gone, and how terrible it could have been, but today has given her the certainty that she is not in control of her own life. Behind her, in between the sound of the waves, she hears Ray talk so affably to the cab driver that they could all be old friends.

They are all just chatting now, Ray is pointing at

something and laughing to himself, and when the driver pulls off, the passengers are all smiling and waving at Ray.

These few days since Glendalough have had one effect on them, to represent love as something that changes a person; not just plans but your entire past; to live for one thing, you must abandon the other. And it comes to her that when you fall in love with someone, you are supposed to fall in love with yourself, too.

June never thinks of Venice.

The gondoliers came across like hoodlums, something that appealed to June; this was how husband no. 2 appeared to her.

Signing the register at the Hotel Fantasia was further proof they were married. And June can remember where the baby they never named was conceived, and how.

Their room was remarkable for its goal-post sized fireplace, which that night had been piled high with wood and set alight with great ceremony. The squalling fire hissed in harmony with their lovemaking.

June blotted the sweat from her chest and followed the flames up the chimney and, if she didn't then wonder what would happen to her and husband no. 2, this was just how life seemed to be going.

Evenings were spent looking out of the long windows at the lagoon, the fast clouds and incomprehensibly happy couples pausing on the Riva below them. In the room there were churchy candles and all kinds of enchantment. They basted each other with hard-to-find perfumes, reminders of the lovely pointlessness of love.

They began to luxuriate in the feeling, marvelling at the clock-towers.

Golden doors at waist height.

Immense, strange basilicas.

A glittering wellhead.

Crossing little bridges on their walks, and bigger ones.

They were so absorbed in each other—staring at their own reflections in puddles, in the backs of spoons—that one afternoon they found themselves in an out of the way square that was swaying with water.

The flood was past their knees, and they hadn't noticed.

They hadn't heard the sirens.

Ray spends his first night at June's on the couch. He'd rather be there than in the spare room, he says.

She can hear him up in the night. Moving around. Being quiet.

She's the old miser lying awake waiting for someone to come in and wake her up.

The sun comes up and she wonders where he is, and she doesn't want to be rude, but if someone is going to stay over would they not adjust to their new environment? A person is an object, and June hadn't reckoned on such a substantial new object in her life, with their hair touching your pillows, their wetness on your towels.

Their and your sound good together.

Their mouth and your mouth.

Your tree, their swing, your tree, their name carved on it.

Your tree and their sap.

She's not exactly thinking straight.

When Ray knocks to say he's off, bye for now, June shouts out bye then.

She gets up and goes to work.

It isn't until she is halfway through Tessa's upstairs bathrooms—cleaning a loo with a view (doing your business under the great authority of bay)—that it occurs to June: what it is like to love, and what it is like for the other person, what it is like to be on the other end.

Perhaps Ray was expecting June to be affronted—and he asked her to come on this trip to Venice anyway—and once upon a time she might have been. But even more than the shock at discovering herself as his friend, Ray has tried to let her be.

He has, she's seen him try.

Has she done the same for him?

Tessa expects June to clean around her. She can be in the bed, and she will want June to carry on with her work, which June has tried to do using Ray's old Discman and headphones, but Tessa likes her to be available for discourse.

Tessa is an asker not an answerer of questions. She has never said what it is she does. Non-disclosure, Tessa said. Being paid not to work? June said. Being paid not to talk, Tessa said.

June is angry and happy about Venice. Can you be those things at once, Tessa asks? I most certainly can, June says.

—It wasn't a good idea, Tessa says. Let's agree on that, for Ray's sake. But was it a very, very bad idea? It depends on what you're angry about. Assuming you're a bit annoyed that he didn't involve you in the arrangements? I would be. Assuming you're a little apprehensive about going back to Venice? I would be. Assuming you're wondering what it's going to be like going away with him? I would be. And you've told him all about you and your husband and he doesn't seem to think that's worth taking into account. I don't know why. Assuming he isn't in some way preoccupied with your husbands? He could be. But there's another question. Do you know how many invitations I've had to go anywhere lately?

—That's why I'm angry and I'm happy, June says.

—More complicated, which makes it easier. You can ignore sense altogether.

Venice is fascinating, isn't it? Tessa says. Fascinating, yes. What do you think going back there will feel like? Angry, happy? More happy than angry, June says. Begin with that, Tessa says. You might find some other feelings. Such as? Fascination. Confusion. Excitement. You might be overwhelmed. You might be comforted.

Tessa, moving from the bed to the bath, wants to know the most comforting place in June's home.

—My bedroom window, looking down on the garden.

—How often do you stand there?

—A lot, June says.

—How often?

—I wouldn't like to think.

—And then what do you do?

—I might have a bath, June says.

Why is this not strange? Talking about your bath to

133

someone in their bath is only what you do when you are on the verge of doing something reckless. And June does not mind what Tessa does. It's her house.

—And then what do you do?

—I'll go to bed, June says. Then I'll go to work.

—Can you do any of that in Venice?

—I don't know. Not really, no.

—No?

—No, June says.

—But you can when you get back.

8

Venice, then

A bit of fog is just the kind of thing to make Venice that more interesting. Perfect sense that they should be sailing towards one of the most famous skylines in the world and not be able to see it.

The shroud creates mystery, and when it comes down to it, Ray says, fog is just a cloud that's touched the ground, it's just a lot of droplets.

June has already booked them tickets for the Doge's Palace. There it is in the distance, coming and going, you can see it—Venice is it—for a moment and then it's enclosed, the fog withholding more fog.

Hotel Castello comes highly recommended. Piero, the owner, revels in the old-time squalor, the *Corto Maltese* prints hung on antler hooks, the soggy floors, his oak table, thick as a pavement, where he's laying out flowers before curving them into something as decisive as a

135

severe haircut, ushering stray stalks, buds and thorns into colourful piles.

Piero gives June some old daisies to take upstairs.

The room smells of bridles and turpentine, and they know without having to check that the antiques are real, not to mention the mildew.

They have three days here.

The lamplight is so dim, the window frames are the size of church doors, and fog squashes into every crevice of them; it's hard to know what's keeping it from coming inside.

But it might be a good thing if June doesn't get to see anything of Venice.

She can go home without anything being stirred up.

She does not want this morning to be about husband no. 2, who spoke like Piero does and who sighed and breathed through his nose a little like Piero does, and who would have made very little of Ray; a thought that travels to a certain destination, not the one she is in now, and not one which would ever have permitted June Wylie to see this as a true friendship.

June and Ray are now sleeping in the same bed, and some days it is good and some days it isn't, things work, or they don't.

She gets into the bed, she is so close to him, and June loves Ray's skin next to hers, his hands, trembling and warm, and the warmth flowing from them.

Tonight it's nice, tonight it works.

Sometimes she stays awake after he falls asleep, just to be there with him for longer.

He's sleeping on his back with his arms above his head, like a child, or as if in surrender. The vulnerability helps June see her own, and be at peace with her own, and she knows she is at peace with it because this feels so different from all those years and years ago. It doesn't feel better, but it does feel easier.

June sleeps for about two days straight.

It's all gone, she thinks when she awakes. The fog hasn't lifted, but they want to make the most of their time.

They'll luxuriate in the damp air.

Downstairs, Piero has arranged food all over the lobby: walnuts, quinces. June and Ray eat jam spread onto toasted sweet brioche.

Breakfast is about fifty euro, and you can get this kind of thing at home, but June feels the weight of the fruit, she rubs the tablecloth between her fingers.

Very, very old.

Would this be beautiful enough for husband no. 2?

She has become so used to other people deciding what is, and what isn't, beautiful with a capital 'B'. Old daisies, the wrong honey, none of it would make the cut.

Ray wouldn't make the cut. But just seeing him get so involved in the jam, just seeing him occupy the day— every day, not just today—fills June with the desire to smell and see and taste things for the first time.

She doesn't care to understand why Ray wouldn't pass husband no. 2's test or why he has passed her test, but it has something to do with how she has ended up back here, not quite under her own steam, but in a new way of being that allows her to decide for herself what is and isn't acceptable; with an emphasis on the 'b' and the 'e' in beautiful.

Yesterday's flower stalks left out on the table like they're part of breakfast.

A napkin heavier than all the others you will ever use.

The victory of powdery soap and people-smells against mildew smells.

The fact that it's not even November, and Piero has the crib out, minus the baby Jesus of course. Does the crib ever get put away? And what was it that happened—long ago, she supposes—that made Piero live in this way? Filling darkened hallways with flowers that no one will ever see, giving coffee and grappa to the bin-man.

You don't make espresso for the bin-men at home. You don't spend fifty euro on breakfast.

The fog is almost too thick to walk out into, but it's their holidays and they want to go for a spritz, June wants to try one, so they walk in the copper light, avoiding the most popular thoroughfares.

In one cafe on a corner by the old shipyard, an old waiter, someone their age, eats his lunch like he has all the time in the world.

His tie has been flipped over his shoulder, an inch of wine in a glass.

He half-fills a bowl from a tureen.

He tastes the rice and sets down the spoon. Ray isn't an expert on soup, if he was, he'd have to think about it more, but he doesn't think this is because this guy is particularly sensitive to heat, but because he was very aware of the taste of things.

Now Ray wants to eat more slowly, too, and, watching this man from the shadows, he and June reach an understanding.

This is where they want to eat, but they'll walk around the block first.

The café is right across from the Arsenale, and Ray gets to pluck out some useful information.

Eleven hundred and something.

In their day, these yards produced a ship a day. Imagine that, the frame, the fit out and the cabins, all in one go. The boats looked like they were carved from the one tree.

And wood is never just wood, so the boats were living things.

Thousands and thousands of people at work on the same ship that, by the end of the day, would be off out to do something like defending the territory or what have you. Something sad about all that beautiful wood being sent off to war.

To the passing observer (someone just off another boat, say), that's thousands and thousands of folk working with a common purpose, so many livelihoods dependant on making such beautiful machines: beauty, ingenuity, craftsmanship, dedication, death, grief, history, stories.

If the fog doesn't clear, this might be all they see of Venice.

It's all giving Ray an appetite.

When he comes to their table, the little speck of

something on the waiter's shirt is a sign for June to ask him what he had for lunch.

A simple rice with peas.

It's not on the menu but they can make it for her if she wants. It's not a risotto and the peas are frozen, but it's very nice.

—*Risi e bisi*, Ray says.

No, that's in April. This a simple rice with peas.

Enough has gone awry in their lives for them to be grateful for the small mercy of a busy man asking the kitchen to make them something simple to eat.

They order a little wine, too, and they eat their first course, a big jumble of ham and things.

Out on the little piazza, the owner of the restaurant has moved from her perch behind the cash register to feed some cats. She sets out several bowls, and the cats move from one to the other like they are eating courses in the restaurant.

The cats depart without much of a thank you.

—It's their birthright as Italians, Ray says. A good meal at a fair price.

And it's a good sign, in a place as touristy as this, to have found a place with its regulars.

—How long do you think it will take us? June says. To get accepted.

—We may have a head start, Ray says. Our age. They know we can't walk that far to go anywhere else.

—Captive audience, June says.

—Fine by me, Ray says. Am I allowed say you look beautiful today?

—This once, June says.

They are sitting at right angles to each other, and Ray has moved his seat, not so that they are touching but so they can feel a little warmth from each other. If it felt like they made love last night, in the bony old bed, in the mould, Ray wants to understand how that was love then and this is also love now.

Perhaps he never got around to enough of it.

—Were you saving yourself? June says.

—Just a bit shy, he says. I didn't know how to ask. I don't suppose you ever had to look very far, it came for you?

—It came for me, is right. It was like being chased around by a pack of dogs. And then it stopped. The dogs moved on.

—Do you miss it? he says.

—Bits of it, she says.

—Which bits?

—The bits I was good at.

—What were they?

—The parts of it I enjoyed, June says. There's no logic to it. You know as much as I do.

—I don't think so, Ray says.

One of them wonders why. Why is this one better than other ones? It's not just the lunch, it's not just the nice rice.

If there was a machine you could plug in, it could sit there in the restaurant, like a sideboard (they could set delph on top of it) and it would give a read-out when you've had a half glass of wine or some of someone else's pudding.

What would the read-out say now? Would it give a reason for their happiness today?

A good sleep in a new bed. Someone to bring your breakfast to you. That's just the absence of struggle, June says. Not unhappy. But isn't that just relief? Ray says. She thinks relief and disappointment are the same thing. Life could be worse but why isn't it better?

They're as well not thinking about it.

Lunch goes on, Ray is eating his as slowly as he can.

He's never too old to learn. They're both doing it; so that she can make the moment last, June is counting the peas in her bowl.

Who counts their peas?

Who lifts a single grain of rice on a tine of their fork?

The white rice and the white tablecloth and their pale hands entwined.

The sky is completely thick with cloud, indicating that Venice has given them a cloak to wrap themselves up in.

They haven't seen enough of it for the place to get a bit much, but June knows it can be a bit much, so the thing to do, if Ray can manage it, is to take a stroll in the Biennale Gardens before turning for home.

It isn't that June wants to talk about husband no. 2, but he liked to find unusual ingredients to put in their drinks. Most of the time this amounted to clogging up your gin & tonic with basil leaves, but one day he remembered a rosemary bush by the monument at the long avenue by the gardens. All their day needed was a waft of herb in it. Not very typical, he'd say, but very simple.

Of course, they didn't see the rosemary, they couldn't find the rosemary, they couldn't get their hands on any, June doesn't think there was any rosemary, anyway, and from that day on they were never allowed to mention the word again.

It takes them hours to get anywhere that's not very far on the map. But there's a nice avenue of trees, as June remembers, and there'll be a bench to rest on.

Usually, the gardens are as busy as a fairground, but today the place is completely deserted. On the bench across from them, a teenage couple are sitting so that they look to have sunken inside their coats.

The girl, who is little bigger than a whippet, shouts something.

—Stupid thing, June says.

—Leave them be, Ray says.

They laugh between themselves—this might not be the best way to react—and June is sure that will be the end of it, but the kids have stood to attention and a moment later one of them throws a stone that hits Ray in the leg.

June can't see. There might be passing traffic at the other end of the avenue; there's a stop for the water buses to dock on their way to the airport.

They start walking to the mouth of the avenue.

More stones scuff the ground towards them.

Kids laughing, kids throwing stones, there's a way to make that cute.

Another scream and June turns around to see the boy and girl walking quickly towards them, as if intending to return a dropped glove or purse.

—Cosa le hai detto? says the boy to Ray.

Side by side June and Ray stand, like figurines on top of a wedding-cake. If they had their wits about them, they could run for the waterfront or call out to the people there.

The boy is tugging at the waistband of his tracksuit pants for something. He feigns to walk away then reaches over to touch Ray's face; nothing much more than that, a stroke on the cheek is all it is.

The girl is leaning forward, close enough to kiss Ray, which is what she tries to do, June is certain this is what the girl is doing, except her eyes are on the boy who, again with an element of tenderness, has Ray's cheeks between fingers and thumb.

The girl is going through Ray's pockets. They must have already decided that June is harmless.

Of course, this all part of the plan.

They've done something wrong; Venice has done this to them. The plans began with those warships in eleven hundred and something, it's impossible to avoid. If only they had stayed behind for another drink at lunch; they would have taken a different way back to the hotel, they would have gone straight home.

The girl has Ray's phone and from his wallet she skims away anything that isn't a card or cash.

June sees a chance to tackle the girl, but she is struck by a blow to the face, which knocks her down and cracks a tooth.

For a moment everything seems calm. The whole thing is over.

June gets to her feet and attempts to walk before falling.

A second passes, another, before she pulls herself together and gets to her feet.

June is too close to see exactly where the young boy has hidden the razor, it must come from the waistband he's been adjusting, but the boy—he can't be more than fifteen—slashes Ray from the side of his mouth to his ear.

A good threshold for pain, it's not something Ray Draper's ever had to be proud of. It takes all his powers of thought not to think, and it is only when he puts a hand to his face that he knows what has happened.

The blood is pouring into his mouth and staining his teeth like he's burst some capsule or other.

The boy is up on his toes (he is not even old enough to shave), the blade's between forefinger and thumb, and June thinks he is going to flick it away but the boy sets off with his hand held aloft, and June is trying to get a proper glimpse of him, so she'll able to describe him, and his hand with the blade in it is floating above his head, what an awful picture.

Ray is an awful picture, too. The girl has the audacity to return, to spit at him—the phlegm is a terrible colour— and throw his emptied and torn wallet in his face.

He has the sense to press the banks of the wound together with his two hands, but his face been turned inside out and taken apart, it looks like it is rotting, June sees how bad it is, and every time she says his name or goes to see to him, Ray shuts his eyes.

Every time he looks at her, June's eyes are fixed on him.

—Ray, she says, and he moves away.

*

The police and ambulance arrive simultaneously from opposite directions before docking and approaching the scene far too slowly for June's liking.

It's the proverbial guilt of one who has come away from a knife-fight with a broken tooth.

This continues in the ambulance boat, where Ray murmurs only a little as the paramedic flushes and glues the wound, and June listens to him recall the incident for the policeman, omitting anything—the stroke on the cheek, for instance—that could be seen as getting in the way of the point, which, for June, is that sooner or later, this was going to happen, it is just unusual but lucky somehow that what is now happening to her is happening in a boat on its way to the emergency room of a foreign hospital.

June's a little light-headed, since you ask, but no more than you would be after seeing your loved one getting their face carved in half.

She asks for a drink of water, but there is none to give her.

No water in a boat in a lagoon?

June would like to get up and move around but she can't really move without upsetting everything. They'll be at the hospital soon, and there'll be a row of helpful faces, and she might even walk this off, she can just go up and down until Ray gets taken care of.

If someone notices her, if they think she looks a bit queasy, or even if they ask her to take her seat, then June can tell them that she isn't feeling well.

She is murmuring now. If someone was lip-reading,

they would see that June is saying, say something, you should say something.

She looks around for some water, even though the paramedic has told her only moments ago that there isn't any, June is thinking she can't blame him, they're busy, and maybe she is being let off the hook here, she should really focus on Ray, he's right there, although he mightn't be, her vision is a bit strange, the lighting has gone a bit arty, and the chances of him knowing how bad she's feeling are very slim anyway, and the last thing June wants to do is get in the way of the emergency services while they're working, so she waits and now she is unable to raise her arm to wave to one paramedic, who is speaking to the other paramedic, and has no idea that June can't move or can't speak but she has to get someone's attention somehow, it might shake things up if she fell over, but she can't even do that, she is just about able to breathe in without any difficulty, she can't do much in the way of breathing out, or in response to the look she gets from the paramedic who decides all of a sudden, this late in the day, to find a little bottle of water and hand it to her, and it might be the tastiest beverage in all of Venice, and June wouldn't disagree, she can't anyway, and she can't do a thing to apologise for the fact that she has dropped the water and the bottle is rolling around at the floor of the ambulance, at the foot of the paramedic, who can see all too well what is happening, and what has caused June to collapse like that, it isn't looking good, the pictures are not good ones, and there is no sense that June is breathing, and if you die of a heart attack, can you die that quickly?

Do you go at once?

It would be a mercy if she does, and if life is so bitter and ridiculous for that to befall June Wylie here, not even at home in her own bed, not even in the mouldy old hotel, in something approaching comfort, couldn't she go in some kind of peace, it is the least she deserves, not to die here, on a boat in front of all these strangers who may or may not, some of them, be highly trained medical profession-als, and she can't hear anyone, can she, she certainly can't hear Ray, but at least there is someone to hold her hand and talk to her, and if she lives, she will have to make it up to him—for those kids—and that is good, she will do that, and June doesn't want to die (it's been a long time since she has been so sure of anything), and whatever goes on here, they have been having a nice time on their hol-idays, and she and Ray can still do all the things they did today, they can keep an eye on each other, and whatever goes on, they have each other, and that is good, because not everyone has someone.

The people in Venice get a hard time for themselves. But those fellas in the ambulance are quick movers, they pull off June's shirt like she is Superman or Tarzan or one of those.

Only the ambulance man, who is doing something complicated with June's chest, says anything.

—*Sta male*, he says.

June's being so quiet, Ray's never seen her be so meek.

As soon as the boat lands, they lay her flat on the ground.

There is a sense of people averting their eyes, swallowing their pity, wondering what it is this sad creature has done to get herself in such a mess.

Is this how it is going to be or is it going to get worse?

It seems easier to think it won't get worse.

The crowd around them is for her not for him, and it contains the prospect of June being picked up from where she lays, taken to the business end of the hospital, wheeled straight to an operating theatre, or abandoned in a corridor before making the short trip to the morgue.

She is taken one way and Ray another.

The hospital is a giant, overcrowded cruise ship. The doctor who admits him looks like he is flicking through bills.

Ray's had the pills they can give him, and they say his face will ache for a while—Faceache Draper—but he has a little curtained off cubicle, and the cubicle has a little window.

The first nurse he speaks to, Paola, is in and out like she is preparing the room for new guests at a B&B.

Paola hasn't heard anything but she'll ask.

She looks at Ray's chart and says, —*Bel viso.*

The words have enough warmth and mockery in them to make him feel less alone, but no less buffoonish for having been stabbed in the first place.

Ray makes a list of all the people he loves. He doesn't know what else to do.

When he sees June, he'll let her know how short the list is.

He has no idea if June is alive, and he is not quite saying to himself he has no idea what to do if she is dead.

He is going to sit in his cubicle and wait. He's trying not to think of his face. Those thoughts would empty you.

He felt the air move through his head.

The sharper the blade the cleaner the cut, he is grateful for that. Good tools, good skills.

Good gestures, loose wrists.

The pose makes the action.

He doesn't see Paola again and it's a night and a day before he's told what's going on.

It's a bypass.

It's happening just now.

That feels very final, very hasty.

He calls Carla and he gets Aileen.

Carla calls him back, it sounds noisy wherever she is, but she doesn't say where she is. She tells Ray not to worry, they are covered, June is and he is, and Ray is to stay where he is and do what he's told.

Ray wants to know what's going on.

Well, Carla knows all about the heart and its bad behaviour, and if Ray wants information, she can give it to him but is there any point in knowing more than you have to?

It's been two days, and it's going to be another week, Ray says. He doesn't have the money for another week.

Carla will have Aileen book flights. Are you allowed to do that? Ray asks. I can do what I want, Carla says.

And one last thing before she goes.

He can only do so much, but Ray must keep functioning. Has he eaten, has he slept? Just do that.

Keep functioning. Be there when June wakes up. She will be weak; she will need more help than you can give.

Carla knows what she is taking about it, and Ray is to listen to her, and that is all he wants to do, but he begins to cry, in the cubicle, on his phone, and people are coming and going, and they leave him be.

Ray's been told to go home and come back again. But they didn't say when, and, if it's Monday—and it is Monday—they were supposed to check out of the hotel this morning.

Ray asks for directions to the Hotel Castello. It's fifteen minutes, that way.

That way could take an hour, it could take all day.

The main way in and out of the hospital is an entrance and a half. It's some gallery in Florence or Rome, or Venice even. The stone is smooth and looks soft enough to lie down on, and the walls lean in slightly, the way they can do, and the light comes in very softly and tactfully.

Perhaps, if you came in this way, you'd hold yourself a bit more upright, you'd think again about being sick, you just would.

And Ray has had it with sickness.

Had it with hospitals.

Had it with Italians.

Had it with beautiful entrances to Italian hospitals.

Had it with life being a dream; and love has become a dream again, June has become a dream.

The one dependable thing in life is that everything is

unexpected. It seems to know everything there is to know about Ray Draper, including how to trip him up at the moment he least expects it, and for him to recognise the feeling inside as emptiness, which has not been caused by the possibility of June dying, but the recognition that you never possess someone, or have what it is you think you gave each other, and the emptiness is not only part of who you are, it's the essence of who you are, and every relationship you have with another person is a reminder of it, and the nature of the relationship doesn't matter, the person is not significant, it's stupid even to believe it will change, you can give yourself to the material truth of their existence and be grateful they are no longer a feature of your imagination, and as long as you don't misunderstand them, those fantasies, in their way, are as deep and sustaining as the body asleep beside yours, and in the end the misunderstanding can be just as substantial, too, because for as long as can Ray can remember, the appearance of love counts as love, it's been that clear, and what is more real to him about June is her soul, and what he sees is her soul, that's the love part of love, their existence, their presence, your memory of them, your ideas of them, and how they are; but perhaps that is not what he is holding onto here, it's not love that he is worried about losing, because June could die today and he would not see himself as anything other than lucky, yes, lucky, because everything that has happened to him since he met her, even ending up in this hospital, can count as that, every encounter has been a lucky one, and the reason he is lucky has nothing to do with whether June will be well or not, and it's not the prospect of being alone again, it's what has happened to his soul, that's what all this is, and it's why he's come down here, to understand what it's like to be with June when she is not there.

Ray is functioning, and the machines by the bed are ticking over, and the air conditioning is blowing a gale.

He's been given the impression that he shouldn't make himself too much at home, but he's allowed to sit by June's bed long after other visitors have been sent away. He's been told not to touch her, so he strokes the metal rail of the bed instead. He doesn't know if this is holding onto her too tightly or not enough.

The room is filled with pools of light. Ray tries to keep talking to June, but he's not a great talker unless there's someone to bounce off.

No one seems to mind that he scrubs himself in the loo, but he can't help but think that June would be appalled if she knew Ray was just sitting there gawping at her.

Every time June opens her eyes, they flicker in surprise, then they are still, giving him the once-over. Only when he's seen her like this, does Ray conclude that making friends in the way that they have might have been different for June than for him, and harder for her than for him, and better for her than for him, and that these past few weeks have been as good as he is ever going to get it.

It might be the longest he's had alone with her face. It's a bit sorry for itself. That tooth, he doesn't want to think about what happened to her, but if anyone was going to lose teeth, he'd prefer if it was him. People are going to be turning away from Ray, as it is.

And this is all taking his mind off his face, anyway, no one has asked him about it, he doesn't know if they know what they know, but something tells him everyone knows.

He sleeps for a few minutes at a time in the chair and, if Ray is sitting still, the light is moving, and every few hours or so, something in the room begins to shine.

Perhaps something glorious is waiting for them.

When Ray gets her home, there'll be a lot more of this. The purring awake from naps like this one, the pair of them tucked up, cuddled up, their only worry being the redefinition of the concept of lying low.

She's awake now and he sits in close, whispering.

—Any pain?

—What a question, she says.

—It would be good to know.

—Feeling no pain, June says. Tell me a nice story. Something with a happy ending.

—How about something with a funny beginning?

—Or that, she says.

He has just the story for her. —The day we met on Tivoli Road, in the rain.

—That was a nice one, she says.

—The big messy hedge.

—I love that hedge.

—I hadn't had the best of days up till then. You didn't look the Mae West, either, in fairness, but it was every disaster rolled into one. Not like this one. More of a homegrown, self-made disaster, another type of disaster altogether. You know my friend Timbo? The little fella.

Future champion of the world. Brilliant enough to hold his own against anyone. But he asked me to be his doubles partner in the last tournament. Sentimental reasons, you have to assume. Let's call this the one big mistake of his life so far, thinking I'd be up to it. He should have known better, I should have, but only I—perhaps you and I—know how thick I can be, and I could have said no to the invitation, of course. You'd think the way I walk would be the giveaway. My running's worse, it doesn't even count as running. It was impressive, not hitting one ball in, not one. And my knees are still sore. My knees are worse than my face.

Ray feels his hand being held, her hand around his thumb, it's soft as that kiss on Tivoli Road. He'll keep functioning. It won't take much, once you brace yourself against the thought that you're only alive if they are.

—Why was it so bad? she says.

—Because I'm really shite at tennis.

—I thought you were supposed to be good.

—No, I'm shite, and I've no knees. I gave them all a laugh, anyway.

—Everyone laughs at you, she says.

She's just woken up or she's about to go to sleep. Does that mean she's better or worse? She'll be glad when that's cleared up. She'd like to know what's expected of her now.

Ray's being so cheerful, poor thing. Give him a top hat and a cane, putting on the Ritz.

He's been crying, hasn't he? The pet.

She may have to get him to go over a few of the details.

Is it bad?

Very bad?

How bad?

Very, very bad?

Ray's been talking to her so nicely.

It's very, very isn't it?

If she could go home now, they could carry on like a bit like this. Him there and her here. Once she gets used to all the lying down and the little efficiencies.

The toilet, how's that happening?

Food? Not much of that seems to be going on. Those tubes don't have rice and peas in them.

That's the nice part of the story.

Nice thoughts won't stick.

She doesn't like lying there, and she doesn't like them looking at her, she doesn't even like Ray looking at her, and she doesn't like pain, and she doesn't like drugs but she can't manage to say so and she is having to put up with an awful lot of what she doesn't like. The fog and the cold and the blood and the bitter wind she felt when they laid her down on the ground to die.

There was pressure, a weight pressing down on her. Sirens went off, sirens for June, but her part in it was quite understated, she feels, almost tasteful.

Yes, she is feeling witty.

She's thinking of them walking out of here in the sunshine. If she is where she thinks she is, there's a lovely square not far from here. Depends on how long she's been here for, and how long they're keeping her in, but it might be spring, soon, and it might be the time for spring kinds of things.

Ray can play tennis in Venice.

Bare legs, June wants her legs out, and her toes. What's the worst that could happen if she got her feet out now?

It's getting a little floaty, alright.

If something very, very bad is going to happen, it would be good to get it over and done with. There's time enough for not living, and not wanting to, which was what June wanted for so long but it's not what June wants now, and listen, Ray is talking now, but he might want to slow down a bit, and speak up, because she can't hear what he is saying, and she won't remember it, anyway, Ray, Ray!

Be quiet for one minute, I've an idea.

Instead of sitting there moping, instead of sitting there like you're at mass, why don't you go outside and roll in some puddles.

Bring me in a stick.

I'm tired of looking at you, no, I'm tired of looking at you here.

Go over to the window so I can look at you over there from over here. Now, go on, go on out the door, I'll follow you in a minute, I'll have a little sleep first.

Blow out that candle.

One of them being stabbed and the other one having a heart attack brings Ray and June closer together in the most straightforward way: one of them is in a wheelchair and the other one is pushing it.

Togetherness, when it wasn't a feature of your daily life, is as opaque and abstract as a foreign national anthem.

Now it's practically ordinary, which is why they can hardly believe it.

Ray got Carla to ask the airport people to organise wheelchairs and things; and June is not saying that they should have got one for him, but even with the walkway racing beneath him, the commotion Ray makes of pushing June's chair disguises the fact that his knees are about to give way.

Before they are through the doors at arrivals, June sees Gurjit, and Preet, with a little sign in the same handwriting that she used to advertise the honey.

The flight was late by hours, but everyone waited.

If June knows anything about Preet, they have been there all night. An Irish person would ask them how they are a thousand times, but very quietly Gurjit takes their bags and gets the car and, after one of the most dreadful hours (flittering chest, ICU thoughts, the machinery), they pull into Ray's block of flats.

It looks quite like a hospital.

Gurjit carries their bags across the carpark; and nothing about his goodbye says this is a man who has been put out of his way in the middle of night. June wants to say thanks to Preet. It nearly midnight, and Preet's sitting lifeless in the front seat.

And what would June say anyway? Real friends don't have to announce the fact.

Ray is pulling her along like a schoolgirl, and June is barely able to see where she is going. Nor is he the kind of man to give two hoots about answering the questions you've asked him, but June is entitled to be cautious about a place, if not the person.

When Ray lets her in to his tiny, tidy, cosy, dreamy looking home, with the basket of balls, and all the old racquets, the little hall resembles the hut at the tennis courts.

June peers into the bedroom—single bed, ship shape—and wonders when she can go to sleep, it's almost two in the morning, but Ray bundles her into his little living room, and she is all under its spell: rugs on the arms of chairs, on the backs of chairs, ready for wrapping around you (Ray sleeps in here, more often than not), flickering glasses arranged hopefully.

And you have the wrong man if you expect Ray not to be excited about having her to recuperate at his place. He searches through the cupboards, laughing for June's benefit at the honey that he has not figured out what to do with.

He unpacks the food that Preet brought them, and as he fiddles around in the kitchen, it's clear that whatever it is Ray is doing for her he does for himself, day after day. This is how it has been for them both, and this is the refuge Ray has sought, consoling yet bare as an old boat.

By the sink, there is a pile with one plate and one mug and some nice cutlery. The setting for his breakfast. And what reason does she have for being surprised that Ray has three types of lemon curd?

Of course, Ray has lemon curd, and she does not want anyone making remarks about it.

She will slip away to bed in a minute, but for the moment June will enjoy being here without having to let him know. All her thoughts are about Ray and his, she hopes, not too lonely life here.

Mystifyingly, June is being presented with a piping hot bowl of microwaved dahl.

After a few moments of staring at it, she gets up, pats Ray on the head (you're starving, I'm tired), and moves down the hall to the bedroom and the single bed, where she'll sleep in her hospital socks, the perfect end to the strangest trip, and the perfect end to the night when you have discovered that you both use the one plate and cup and bowl over and over and over again.

She's lying there, too tired to sleep, when she hears music from other room. Something that's far too jaunty for this time of night.

June opens the door an inch, so tired that she is not sure what she is seeing. Ray's dancing with his eyes closed, but she's not falling for that one. He knows she's there. As with everything to do with June Wylie and Ray Draper, this is new and not new.

Ray has not been loved, but he is by her.

The dancing must be something he does. Complicated but simple if you know a jive when you see one. A rock step, and two triple steps, three, a, four, five, a, six. That's as far as Ray gets before it becomes more like some free expression June might be able to join in with. A few months ago, she would have shrunk from this.

—Any requests? he says

—You work away, she says.

—I'll turn it off, he says.

—No, she says. Don't. I think I'm too tired to sleep.

Ray puts something else on and wanders over to her. The music makes its soft approach, too. What sounds good to him sounds good to her.

He lets his eyes close like he's listening to some good news.

The sway comes of its own accord.

If you've lived through thirty years of *Top of the Pops*, miming to music comes naturally. He does the harmonica in the song for a good minute before handing over to June, who carries on until the song fades out before Ray puts it on again and June, who a moment ago was so exhausted she thought she might sink through the bed, starts her own dance. It's like she's sitting up on a horse.

She is wrapped up in the tune, she knows the lines, she'd forgotten them, but she knows them.

—Oh girl, I'd be in trouble if you left me now.

—The Chi-Lites, he says.

—The Chi-Lites!

The song open ups, and in the harmonica notes, the lift in them, the instrument is searching for its place in the song.

Where it fetches up is somewhere else entirely.

Ray puts on a faster one, something old that June doesn't know, and as the notes find each other, he begins doing something with his hands that makes it seem like he is handling hot toast. June has her hand out, pulling him close enough for him to feel the cottony bed and hair smells. As though they have sore backs, they begin rotating side by side, so stiff they can barely scratch their own

161

bellies. Ray resumes juggling the toast and suddenly he could be the man directing traffic in that piazza in Rome, blowing his whistle and twirling. He drops into a crouch, and if you squint, he could be Spiderman spinning out his webs.

9

The walk from my house to yours

Who are they now? Now that June is tucked up in Ray's bed and he's in and out every five minutes to make sure she hasn't died, they are here today.

They are the mint on the pillow. They are the turn-down service. They are breakfast in bed. They are the egg with two yolks. They are the shell. They are some of the best butter in the world. They are the cast iron pan you've had for years.

They are the iron and the furnace.

They are the towel you wrap around yourself when you've burned your hand on the pan.

They are the cold water, the warm water, the hot water. They are the taps and the bath.

They are Radox, Imperial Leather, they are soap when soap was soap. They are toothmarks on the soap, they are foam on your chin, facecloth over your balls, they are private parts, they are pubes, they are the cleanest parts of themselves.

They are fingers, and open palms, the hand turned the other way, they are that's fine, then. They are no hands. They are hands in the air, behind your head or on your waist.

They are the fantasy from that long ago but comes true now. They are what doesn't need fantasising about, they are what doesn't bear thinking about.

They are going to live forever, they are good God almighty the burning fires of hell, they are changing the subject.

They are the for in forever, the never that's not in forever, the ever in the never that's not in forever.

They are gone tomorrow.

June hadn't seen herself as staying long at Ray's, but it's been a week now and soon they'll run out of lentils and honey and what will they do for fun, then?

Quite a few times she's been about to tell Ray how nice it's been.

And she's been giving him some input.

The input includes, you don't have to stop singing when I come in the room. It includes, you don't have to be so careful spreading the honey onto my toast. It includes, you don't have to keep peeking in to check that I haven't died. It includes, try rinsing the shower after you. It includes, don't lecture me about music back in the day, I was there, too. It includes, dry your hair before you go out, you'll catch a death.

And, on his way out, Ray is opening the mail.

He has his concentrating face on, if you didn't know him, you'd think he'd had some news.

He has had some news.

Well, this is a bit much, he thinks.

Not that, not now, that's cruel, he thinks.

Although it is as fitting as anything else Ray Draper has seen lately.

He folds his arms and says, —They're going to do my knees.

Or one of his knees, then the other one, but that's good news, isn't it?

He was on some referral list, he says, but Ray is on so many lists that he wasn't expecting to be notified so soon.

And he's never opening the mail ever again.

It's what June has feared, too. One of them going through an operation so soon after Venice seems like an invitation for it go wrong or for the pair of them to be spectacularly relieved. June can speak for them both when she is not counting on being relieved.

Ray's the same. He's doing fine with the knees he has, on the bike, and the leaning on things, and the sort of trotting; that might do him another while, he doesn't want a new knee if it's going to mean putting them through more hospitals, he'd rather keep the old bad knees than put either of them through another ordeal getting good new ones, or one good new one.

It won't feel right, him having newer new bits than June's new bits.

It'll feel like cheating.

Ray will sort it out.

He'll hop on Raimund, and he'll go and see Carla, and he'll head down for June's mail, too, and he'll pop into the courts on the way.

He's outside and he's on the bike, and he tries to shoo her back inside and June can see it, but he's upset, and she's upset too, because he is, and because one thing about new love is that it makes an awful pessimist of you.

—Liar, she says.

—What do you mean, liar?

—Just saving time. I'll ask you if you're okay and you'll say you are, and I'll say liar. And since we're on the subject, I'm looking at you like you'll be getting on the bike and cycling down there, and I'll never see you again.

Instead of Ray shooing her off, June shoos him off.

The courts are completely empty, and the cabin is open. Ray pushes the door. The other old fella who works there is called Bren, and he's the same age as Ray, and he might as well be Ray, but he doesn't take things to heart the way Ray does.

Ray calls out hello. Bren is reading something fascinating on his phone, and whatever it is he's looking at (astrophysics/kittens on skateboards), Bren's mind is on that and not on Ray.

Ray waits a minute before announcing himself.

Bren waits another minute before replying.

Ray has just one question.

Timbo, has anyone seen him?

—Ah, Bren says.

—Ah, Ray says.

How long was Ray away for?

A couple of weeks.

Well, Bren says, something happened, and Katrina banned them from setting foot in the courts, and they ignored her, and so did everyone else, and that's when Katrina called the guards, and that's when everyone who could went off to join the clubs in Sandycove and Glenageary and took Timbo with them.

—She'd been after them a while, Bren says. People like them.

—People like them?

—I've told her to knock that off.

—Did she wait till I was away? Ray says.

He gets straight on Raimund and wheels down to June's.

Ray's unsettled to think of Timbo existing elsewhere, and he's unsettled that he's unsettled, only because Ray hasn't ever been able to think of Timbo existing beyond tennis.

Perhaps he goes home with his mum, and they're tucking into their tea, something hearty and filling, Mercy makes sure of it, and as if by magic everything and everyone is safe and warm and well. Perhaps.

It is not a good feeling.

When Ray pulls up on the bike, June's house says much the same to him, it says this place means more to her about her life than Ray's little place does to him of his.

But it takes him a moment.

There are two black squares where they used to be.

From the phone in her house, Ray calls June in his house.

—It's me, he says.

—I know, she says.

But June's in a hurry, Tessa's come over with some gifts, and June doesn't want to keep her waiting.

—A couple of things, Ray says. I'm worried something's happened to the bees. I don't know how to say this to you, but the hives are gone.

—Oh, Ray, I'm so sorry, I'm so sorry. I forgot.

She was so worried something would happen to him—people can die of beestings, and Ray is just the type of character who would die from beestings—and that one night she couldn't get to sleep for worrying about it and she called Tommy, and Tommy knows a fella, and he must have taken them sooner than she thought, and she feels terrible for not telling him.

June was just worried Ray would be killed by the bees.

—You're not to worry about that kind of thing, Ray says.

—It's not that easy, she says. I was sure the bees had it in for you.

June tells him about the day Mik Bolger pushed the hives on top of Preet and how that was a lucky escape and ever since then she's worried something like that will happen again. Don't worry, Ray says, but I do worry, she says, it's good to worry, worry is a form of protection, she says. But if I worry about something it goes wrong on me. So now I worry about worrying about you. You did that for me? Ray says. You could have said to be careful. No

168

way that would work, June says. You should see yourself. Cutting off bits of your own fingers. Running into other people's knives. And I've been stung by a bee before, he says, and I've survived. You haven't been stung by hundreds of bees at once, June says. If they were to turn on you, I'd never be able to, I don't know what I'd be able to do.

June only wants to talk about the absolute certainty of Ray being stung to death by her bees.

—You go around like you're determined to have harm inflicted on you, she says.

—June? Ray says.

—Yes? she says.

—I thought Tessa was there.

—She's just leaving.

—Don't you need to go and talk to her?

—She'll be fine, June says.

—What'll you do now you've no bees?

—You're my bees, she says.

The doctor's surgery is shut by the time he gets there, so Ray spins along by the seafront on the way up home. The sunset is happening behind him, and he can see it in the length of his shadow. And the more he thinks of it, the more he thinks that people can put up with anything. People can really put up with anything.

Today, the swimmers at the cove look a little too contemplative, the clouds are lower in the sky, and the sky is lower, and when he gets home, June wants them to talk about his knees.

—There is no hurry, Ray says, but he is not the one setting the pace today.

According to the rules of logic to which June Wylie still adheres, life was supposed to change when they made friends; and of course, it did, but any more than she believes husband no. 2 is in the kitchen making Ray's dinner, she does not believe their bodies go on forever.

She accepts and loves all the things wrong with Ray, and he accepts and loves all the things wrong with her, and June wants him to do his new knee. There's no use in having a moment over it, it's assumed that operations and hospitals are an awful business.

She's so sure of it that Ray feels like he is being sold to. He thinks he can figure out an alternative. Which is staying the way he is.

—Being old reminds you of your options, June says.

He could get one done, then he could get the other one done, or he could get both done, or he could wait, or he could think again, one or the other.

And June does not say that, when you have lived your life the way she has, there is no useful distinction between carefulness and recklessness when they result in the same thing.

—I'll mind you, she says.

—But I'm supposed to be minding you, he says. Who will look after us?

They'll have each other, June says. But Ray is all het up and he makes them dinner, and they do feel very alone now, the pair of them, and scared.

Ray can't think of anything else. Mouthful of Scotch

broth, a think about his knees. A bit of toast, a think about his knees. Soup, knees, toast, knees. Afterwards, he does what he's been told not to do, and he starts to think about what life might be like when he has some new bits for himself.

Just think, he can walk where he wants, they can go where they want.

All the places that aren't Venice sound great.

—The adventures, Ray says.

—Adventures, June says. There isn't much money now, between them, but all the free things sound fun.

Gardening is mostly free.

So are naps.

So is putting on your Sunday best and going down to the cove to watch the stars, which are all a bit dainty, a bit exquisite and self-absorbed, giving off all that light and expecting to be admired for it.

But none of that costs money.

Nor does going back in the morning to laugh at all the eejits doing aerobics on the seafront. Nor does clapping when a seagull steals someone's ten-euro muffin. Nor does thinking about what happens if anything goes wrong in the hospital.

And the more they try to tally it, what is the right way to have gone about it, what is not, the more they think that whatever else it does, love does not take away from life.

Dreams are part of life, Ray, and dreams overflow into life. And if you are not careful dreams can become your life.

Ray is hallucinating trees.

He is support-stockings.

He is chatty nurses.

He is peeing in a bottle.

He is a bit parched.

He is Zimmer to get to the toilet, he is wheelchair to leave the hospital.

He is a talking to from the physiotherapist.

He is sleepy, he is weepy, he is cranky, he is useless, he can tell you why, he is painkillers, he is slow.

He is oven chips, he is cup-a-soup.

He is pottering, he is radio, he is favourite songs, he is no bath, he is smelly feet in those hospital socks, he is a rubbish Santa with smelly feet and no shopping done.

He is too long waiting, he is anything strange or startling, he is what's going on outside, I'd even read a paper, what's going on here, what's going on with you?

What's going on is worry.

What if you meet someone and not want to be away from them, but when you find that you truly love someone, you want to outlive them, so they do not have to outlive you?

June was outside getting something to eat when husband no. 2 died. He'd sent her out for a walk to the Italian cafeteria on Fleet Road.

What kind of person specifies the kind of sandwich you should buy to eat by their death bed? Husband no. 2 was right, as usual. Very nice people, very good sandwiches. But someone decided to remake June's food—they'd forgotten the pickle and mortadella likes pickle—and when she got back to the hospital he had gone.

Love is someone sending you out for a proper sandwich, so you don't have to watch them go.

Love is having someone wash your feet because they smell and they need washing and you're not able to do it for yourself, and because they might want to mind you.

June and Ray become very adept at washing each other's feet.

Some very good work goes on in between the toes.

It's not just that they're still ticklish, it's the feeling of being children (being silly, and silliness not being silly) and the understanding that comfort can come from anywhere, and anyone, and every now and again the past will happen to you, entering you unawares. This includes the patient young man in his own anorak at vespers, and the happy woman stirring the mix for a fruitcake.

That's all the past has to say for itself now. You can shape your lives around avoiding certain memories and using only certain parts of certain memories. The book of your life is for flicking through, it's been dropped in the bath.

He is not the kind of man to feel injured by the world, and he is fucked if he is the kind of man to resign himself to the whims of the fates, for the fates don't care for the likes of Ray Draper.

He is not the kind of man to reduce the size or scale of a task in hand, but the recuperation side of things doesn't come easy.

Whenever she comes in from work, June smells of outside. Ray asks if he can smell her jumper; he can tell the weather from it, and is awestruck, just a little, to be close to her.

The snap has gone right out of him.

He holes up inside himself.

The last he saw of the bay, it was swollen and grey and sad-looking, and he wants to see it bright again. Another crack at the pier, June on his arm, out and back again on foot. He wants that much. Never once does he think of the past—seventy odd years of age and there'll be no more listening for God, the mind only found itself in piss-houses, lonely cans of orange.

He's had no experience of God in his life at all.

And by that recognition and by an eerie force of will the thoughts of a lifetime find themselves disentangled.

Ray Draper feels himself operating under instruction.

The message is: live each day.

He wants to live each day. He wants to live them with her.

Six o'clock in the morning, and June pulls open the curtains. The light feels different when you're about to go out in it and today they're going to walk from his house to hers.

Last night they heard a van pulling off and, when June went to the door, there was a family bag of Opal Fruits sitting on the mat.

This was Tommy saying good luck.

They've been doing their training—they're devout

at all that, Ray's praise for June giving up smoking, her worries that he'll twist his knee by standing in a pothole, her praise for his patience, and his worries that it's been too long for someone to be cooped up minding someone else.

Ray's in the bathroom and June's in the hall, looking in. They go quietly through their morning, the carefulness moving around them like the steam.

They've been doing a lot of this.

Ray's hair is soaking the back of his t-shirt, there's toothpaste in the corner of his mouth, and the scar, that's there, but he looks just fine to her.

Look at me, he's been saying.

Don't, he's been saying.

Oh well, he's been saying.

It's okay to not talk about everything, he's been saying.

Not talking can be as good as talking.

I'll keep some things to myself, sometimes you have to.

But as far as today is concerned, they have only to get themselves out the door, and along Tivoli Road, sweet old Tivoli Road, and, if they're feeling good, perhaps they'll swing past the tennis courts, and they might run into someone (Ray doesn't really know where Timbo is), then start to get themselves settled at June's.

She has figured its nine months since they met at the Sari Grocery.

June's been in and out, for the company and for all the spicy food Ray can't do without. This means sometimes they eat separate meals, but they agree on dessert—the sweet tooth on her since she left off the rollies—and it's not just the kulfi and the Indian desserts, it's the craving for a Mars bar (she cuts them up and puts the slices on a plate) and the Yorkies that Ray devours like he wants rid of them.

It's almost as if June thinks she should make them something for the journey—it's a twenty-minute walk—and it feels like negligence not to. It would be a pocket full of sweets, essentially, and it's not how they will be going on.

Carla has given them lists, a firm talking-to in bullet points, and there is something good and trustworthy about a note pinned to a fridge door, which says: if you do these things, other things will take care of themselves.

It's been no surprise to see Ray, the caretaker, being so careful with his exercises.

Good boy, very obedient, but he does need a little help getting his shoes on.

She's going to stop short of doing his laces for him.

She does his laces for him.

—Do you think we're up to this? he says.

—Don't be doing that to me now, June says.

And they hear themselves be noisy in the hall, usually it's one or the other, and Ray's front door is open, and June stands back to let him go through it, and how they both suddenly want to talk about the hospitals they've been in, and the nice lunch in Venice, where they let someone else choose for them, and the walk in the park afterwards, and how this is the first time they've been out together since then.

*

The crescent that runs around the estate is always quiet at this time of day. And it might even be the case that the bypasses and new bits are doing their work.

On they go.

But Tivoli Road has something wrong with it, it has one thing wrong with it.

The hedge they kissed under has been trimmed.

Some stray cuttings are sitting in by the wall, and Ray moves fast. June claps her hands when he fills his pockets with leaves.

—Glorious, she says. How long ago was that?

—Years, Ray says.

—At least that, she says. What happens now?

—We're walking, he says.

They are tempted to turn left down on Patrick Street. The Savoy will just be getting going, and they'd be up to some chips and/or Bolognese, but they keep going the way they're going for much the same reason as Ray says he doesn't want to see what's happening at the tennis courts: he's got better things to be doing.

And there is a little something that he would like to do.

Instead of turning down to Eden Villas, and June's house, they could risk a quick detour. So far, Ray's knee has been doing what a knee should do, and the place he has in mind is only ten minutes away.

The clubhouse is like a mansion. They walk in like they own it. It goes without saying that this is June's first time here, even if she's cleaned houses either side of it.

June thinks Ray's outfit means he'll fit right in, which

177

will be why they'll make friends within minutes and be invited to apply for membership, with a lovely spot at top of the waiting list.

All fees waived.

A pair of ladies pause their game of bridge to see who Ray and June are and who they're not. Even by ear, Ray can tell Timbo's practising his serve outside.

He walks onto the balcony. Timbo is on the faraway court, playing with someone near enough his own age. But Ray can barely see them, and they can't see him.

It's cold and it looks like Timbo's all wrapped up, but Ray can hear the balls fly, supersonically.

Feet, drop, swing, all of it at once. If you notice one thing you miss another and Ray takes in Timbo's everything. It's all so nanosecond-glint in your eye, but it's the toss—the arc the ball makes before Timbo hits—that would offer you redemption.

Look, the shots skid in every direction the boy wants them to, one of them he almost gets to stop short, magically.

He is serving so purposefully, faultlessly, composing himself like a matador after each one, moving through the court with absolute clarity minding his feet, moving with more and more intent, until Timbo's gallant opponent joins Ray in admiring him, not as a participant in the game but as another observer of this fluorescent, perfect boy.

Some days the days come and go.

The radio's on low, and the plates from breakfast stay

out, and something in the paper—a factory collapses, killing hundreds; a turtle swims halfway across the world to meet its mother—will delight one of them, or baffle them, or madden them to the extent that tears of absolute incomprehension start pouring out of them, fucks starts pouring out of them, and turn into something like hilarity, then gratitude, then disbelief: why has the world sent them all this news, what are they supposed to do with it, and what did anyone do to end up in a word like this?

The seasons are inverting, systems developing and crashing, people are having to live in wigwams. Except to warn each other of all the things they already knew about, June and Ray can't think of a single thing to save themselves from it.

Here today, gone tomorrow.

So, they go wandering.

All weathers.

Some weathers.

Down past Tessa's they go, always towards the cove.

In a move that June hasn't questioned, Tessa has asked her to work on an exclusive basis, a flexible arrangement at Tessa's discretion that amounts to half the work June used to do for twice the money.

Ready to rumble, Ray says.

Ready to be rumbled, June says.

But Ray hasn't had much luck of his own on the work front. The scar does startle people and probably keeps them from giving him the benefit of the doubt that he deserves.

On they go.

A few doors along from Tessa, a dog has gotten to know their movements. One morning, he just announces himself to them.

That the house has enough security paraphernalia for an embassy gives the dog a certain air of solemnity, grandeur, a certain air of remove.

He's part spaniel, part something else, just like Ray, but June is quick to remark that the dog's liver and white colouring is not as appealing as Ray's.

Perhaps it's the dog's age, but they have already moved through a few stages in their friendship, which is now one of duty and expectation. There's no asking him how he is, but the dog does often seem down in the dumps.

Today of all days, he's keen to join forces.

—Can we call him Placid? Ray says.

—Must we? June says.

—I'd like to, Ray says.

—Why?

—No why, he says.

And that's one of their gifts to each other; maintaining a little bit of the stranger about themselves.

Who's this person in my house? Why are they folding the tea-towels like that? Why are they looking like they might have some affection for me?

There is no one they know at the cove and the place is busy with all sorts running to different schedules.

A concrete bench affords them all the view they need of what goes on. They don't know why no one else ever sits there. Perhaps it's become known as theirs, and the best thing about watching all the bodies and faces, mainly the faces, is that these happy expressions can come home with you. The good morning you've promised yourself can get you through the day, it can pull you from one to the next.

Their next adventure—once Ray has had his other knee done—is something that for so long would have sounded to June like a punishment.

He has read about a nice little bed and breakfast in Bangor, and there'll be afternoon naps just the way they like them, there'll be fish and chips in a place quite like the Savoy but where they don't know you, and walks along a pier shorter than their own, and the loveliest thing about this trip is that they might go on it and they might not.

Itineraries suggested, approved, and agreed, medication ordered, socks and smalls neatly folded, starched, and ironed, why not?

A little money to spend, thanks to Tessa.

It's always good to have options—being there, there, or being there, here. The soul of possibility is enough.

But the dog's not had much luck on the food front, and heads for home before they do, in search of a little conviviality on his own terms, perhaps a little quiet. The swimming side of all of this is getting very noisy and communal.

June has stopped asking Ray if he'll get in this year. She can't find a way of putting it without making him feel bad.

Ditto Ray on June's bees; he wants her to get them back. He'd even been coming around to the idea of honey, a little taste of it as he spreads it on her toast; it's rum, it's butter, it's armpits, it's lips, it's flowers, it's what the bees ate, it's I missed this, it's resin, it's wow it's trees.

Imagine if he'd never noticed the honey in the first place, imagine if Ray had never been declared fit as a fiddle and hadn't chosen to celebrate by popping into the Sari Grocery for a binbag of pakora. Or imagine if Ray had been that bit better at tennis and he'd stayed on at the courts to practise with Timbo. Or imagine if he'd had a fridge full of tasty leftovers to go home to, going mad to Steely Dan. Or imagine if tasty leftovers and going mad to Steely Dan were all Ray Draper had had to feel good about in life and imagine if that wasn't enough.

There's a crowd of men with gleaming faces getting in and out of the water. Some of them are bald, some of them aren't, but they all have the same big bellies and fat backs, and Ray thinks they have to be brothers.

There are sausage sandwiches in a lunchbox, but someone has forgotten the cups to drink whatever is in the flasks, and they are having to pass the flasks around. Ray thinks it's tea, June thinks it's Champagne. No one would be that eager to drink tea from a shared flask.

She's right, Champagne in a thermos flask.

Out comes some champagne in an actual bottle.

You can't really tell what has the brothers so giddy. There is more than one thermos, more than one bottle, and they are all wandering about without getting dried, hugging each other. Everyone gets hugged by everyone else.

It's not entirely celebratory, if you look closely, and it's not entirely commiserative.

They're doing a toast; the toast is to mixed emotions.

They're toasting to positive mental attitude.

They're toasting to brighter futures.

They're toasting to balls, to losing them.

One of the brothers—the fittest of them, very tattoo-y, likely minus one ball—is about to hand the bottle along to the curious old couple.

But the look tells Ray all he needs to know.

Old fella with long hair. Old fella in tennis shorts. Old fella with a dirty big scar.

Ray knows when people are noticing his face, and noticing the noticing makes it worse, because it's happening anyway, so it's fine when he doesn't notice it, because the nice, tattooed brother has noticed it, hasn't he?

He glances over at Ray, and he smiles over at Ray, and he winks at Ray, and Ray knows what all this is getting at.

I've seen you, and you've seen me see you, but I promise you it doesn't matter.

Pity isn't the worst of it.

Can pity be cruel, can it be vain?

Pity can be anything it wants.

The scar has been the end of smiling at people, and it's been the end of the interactions. Ray was more a part of the world then, with all the talking to people. The ones who stare, they don't really want to talk but they do want to ask questions, they want to know what Ray could have done to avoid it, which means, what did he do to deserve it?

Got born, he'd say.

*

It's on strange days like this one that they can't get home quick enough.

They have no need for the mixed emotions of the brothers with gleaming faces; they have enough of their own.

Perhaps it's the same variety of optimism they both held so long ago (her: in a pub in Kentish Town, him: picking strawberries) that they almost don't recognise it. Now, they feel it with an urgency that can only come from it having been transformed from something that is not optimism. Loneliness, now that they've mentioned it once they can't stop.

When June gets the key in the door, and all very distractedly she puts on the kettle for the tea and she cuts up their Mars bar and puts it out on two saucers, they find everything associated with loneliness gets transformed one more time; the end of being alone is not the end of who you are.

That, night, as they're tucked up, Ray shares an idea for another trip, even if it's only a matter of going out so they can come home again.

—Let's go to town, he says.

—In what sense?

—*Town*, Ray says.

—Dublin?

—No, Beijing.

—You don't go into town, June says.

There isn't much to say about why Ray never goes into town. He just prefers it here. A year can go by, and he won't leave Glasthule.

—It might be nice to see what's changed, he says.

Of course, they both wonder about the dog, and if it will want to come on the train, but that mightn't be fair on the dog.

They might be able to find an album Ray doesn't have and wants June to hear. In a record shop or comic shop or book shop, he will discover something he had forgotten he loved, and he will attempt to persuade June of what she doesn't need persuading of.

They might find that in town, and if they don't, they'll come home.

It gives them a thrill to get smartened up to walk down to the Dart as if they are heading into college or a job in a tech firm; and to think everything they have done since they got back from Venice, and since Ray has moved in here, everything they decide on, what goes on the pasta, who sleeps where, can offset the old rawness and the old despondency and that those feelings can't be avoided entirely.

There's a quicker way to the station, but walking through the village, and doing something they never do—paying for a tea to takeaway—allows them to see the commuters who've got the run on them, and to overhear conversations relating to brutish work days and suspiciously complicated commutes, phones and screens held out—in the way cops flashed their IDs on *Hill Street Blues*—to pay for what it is people have for breakfast when they're not at home.

But the scene on the station platform could be set to music, a ballet being performed to a dirge.

Someone is doing lunges.

Someone else is in their pyjamas.

Someone has forgotten something and is going home to get it.

Someone else is down on their haunches, thinking.

Someone else is brushing their teeth.

Someone else is finishing their homework.

Someone else is using their finger to paint a picture of a flower directly onto a screen.

Someone else is asleep standing up. Ray thinks it's one of the brothers with the gleaming faces. Yesterday, at the cove, when June and Ray were taking their leave, one of the brothers held up a bottle, did a cross in the air, and solemnly said, may you live always in mutual charity.

June turned to Ray and said, did he just marry us?

Ray let out his sanest laugh, and said, it wouldn't be the worst idea.

It is an idea, she said.

Isn't it? he said.

Have we not done it already? she said.

We have, he said, we are.

They are.

They are not.

First of all, there is nothing to say that anyone on this platform is living in the same moment as anyone else, or even in the same lifetime, and in the recognition of that fact, there's a slowing.

Time shows its wares. The singing in the wires reveals the cha-cha-cha that everyone keeps to themselves. The way the rails bend, that's the work of the finest pencil drawing. Quick, someone colour in some long grass and some wildflowers, that's what this place needs for itself.

The train pulls in and those in the know wait with saintly faces at the exact spot where the door will fall open for them.

Ray and June squeeze themselves on, and in the tunnel before Dún Laoghaire station, time opens its coat for them, which is to say the clock is now running backwards, and all they'll do today can be previewed in bright pictures.

They'll walk from Westland Row towards Stephens Green and down Grafton Street, veering off towards the old arcade, getting stuck there for too long, stopping off for a bit of lunch, soup and a sandwich, and the seating arrangements working out so beautifully they'll be able to see up and down South Great George's Street.

There is Ray on his way to see *Annie* in the Gaiety. He'll cry.

There he on his way to Golden Discs for his copy of *Moondance*. He'll cry.

There is June on her way to the Coffee Inn where she'll be sick in the toilets and that'll be it for her and drugs. There she is on her way to throw eggs at Richard Nixon.

The occasions line up like pearls on a silk thread, and it could be that that they've met on this street before, many times as a matter of fact, and if there's no knowing what year it is or what day of the week it is, they know that it will always come around to the point where you can move freely through yourself, and in the charisma of the moment, sandwiches will appear without having to be asked for, and how greedily they'll eat them.

The soup, too, is from long ago. You'd taste the decades in it. Onion, carrot, celery, stock cube, the risqué presence of dried herb.

They'll take a wander towards Trinity then, down through the alley with all the jewellery shops, and it's not any old walk is it, they're not on their way for the pints on a Saturday afternoon. June will hear Ray's brain cranking, he'll be about to ask if she'll make an honest man of him, but why would they ruin such a good thing when it's been going so well and they've already given each other all they have, and it'll be a relief to them both when Ray won't seem to make out his own thoughts. He'll think better of it with a kiss on her cheek that says, don't worry I won't, and they'll make it back to Grafton Street, and sure enough, everyone they will want to see will be there, and there'll be a gentle reverberation of some kind, the death of someone widely beloved, or the referendum that makes good adjustments to society's progress, and everyone will be delighted to be sharing the same air, strange to think how long it's been, a minute or thirty years, and June Wylie and Ray Draper will be falling in step in the way they do when they're mindful of one another, which will tell them that it was good to come out, and if it ever occurs to them to go back to town, all of this fascination can be found on the daily commute.

They've only gone out to come back in.

The train has moved on through Monkstown and is halfway to Seapoint and as it gets busier there are calls to move along and they are pushed towards the sea side of the carriage where the bay is docile and the tide is low but different to how it was yesterday at the same time, a little greener, a little greyer, and June has one hand on the rail and the other in Ray's paw, just to steady him.

You'd hardly notice they were there.

A Note on the Author

Andrew Meehan has published three books *One Star Awake*, *Instant Fires* and *The Mystery of Love*. He grew up in Dublin and lives in Glasgow, where he teaches Creative Writing at the University of Strathclyde.